The
Teddy
Robinson
Storybook

For all Families with a Teddy Bear

KINGFISHER
LONDON & NEW YORK

Publisher's Note
The stories in this collection are reproduced in the form in which they appeared
upon first publication in the U.K. by George G. Harrap & Co. Ltd.
All spellings remain consistent with these original editions.

The stories in this collection were first published by George G. Harrap & Co. Ltd.
This collection first published by Kingfisher in 2000

This edition published in the United States in 2010 by Kingfisher,
175 Fifth Ave., New York, NY 10010
Kingfisher is an imprint of Macmillan Children's Books, London.

Distributed in the U.S. by Macmillan, 175 Fifth Ave., New York, NY 10010
Distributed in Canada by H.B. Fenn and Company Ltd., 34 Nixon Road,
Bolton, Ontario L7E 1W2

Library of Congress Cataloging-in-Publication data has been applied for.
ISBN: 978-0-7534-3044-6

Kingfisher books are available for special promotions and premiums. For details contact:
Special Markets Department, Macmillan, 175 Fifth Ave., New York, NY 10010.

For more information, please visit www.kingfisherbooks.com

Printed and bound in the U.K. by CPI Mackays, Chatham ME5 8TD
1 3 5 7 9 8 6 4 2

The
Teddy
Robinson
Storybook

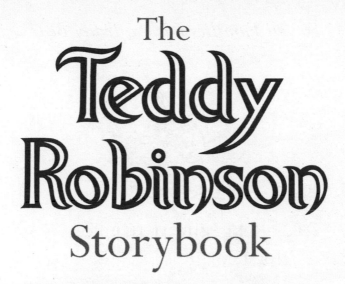

Joan G. Robinson

KINGFISHER
NEW YORK

Contents

Teddy Robinson's Night Out

Teddy Robinson was a nice, big, comfortable, friendly teddy bear. He had light brown fur and kind brown eyes, and he belonged to a little girl called Deborah.

One Saturday afternoon Teddy Robinson and Deborah looked out of the window and saw that the sun was shining and the almond-tree in the garden was covered with pink blossom.

"That's nice," said Deborah. "We can play out there. We will make our house under the little pink tree, and you can get brown in the sun, Teddy Robinson."

So she took out a little tray with the dolls' tea set on it, and a blanket to sit on, and the toy telephone in case anyone rang them up, and she laid all the things out on the grass under the tree. Then she fetched a colouring book and some chalks for herself, and a book of nursery rhymes for Teddy Robinson.

Deborah lay on her tummy and coloured the whole of an elephant and half a Noah's ark, and Teddy Robinson stared hard at a picture of Humpty-Dumpty and tried to remember the words. He couldn't really read, but he loved pretending to.

*He stared hard
at a picture of Humpty-Dumpty*

"Hump, hump, humpety-hump," he said to himself over and over again; and then, "Hump, hump, humpety-hump, Deborah's drawing an elephump."

"Oh, Teddy Robinson," said Deborah, "don't think so loud – I can't hear myself chalking." Then, seeing him still bending over his book, she said, "Poor boy, I expect you're tired. It's time for your rest now." And she laid him down flat on his back so that he could look up into the sky.

At that moment there was a loud *rat-tat* on the front door and a long ring on the doorbell. Deborah jumped up and ran indoors to see who it could be, and Teddy Robinson lay back and began to count the number of blossoms he could see in the almond-tree. He couldn't count more than four because he only had two arms and two legs to count on, so he counted up to four a great many times over, and then he began counting backwards, and the wrong way round, and any way round that he could think of, and sometimes he put words in between his count-ing, so that in the end it went something like this:

> *"One, two, three, four,*
> *someone knocking at the door.*
> *One, four, three, two,*
> *open the door and how d'you do?*
> *Four, two, three, one,*
> *isn't it nice to lie in the sun?*
> *One, two, four, three,*
> *underneath the almond-tree."*

And he was very happy counting and singing to himself for quite a long time.

Then Teddy Robinson noticed that the sun was going down and there were long shadows in the garden. It looked as if it must be getting near bedtime.

Deborah will come and fetch me soon, he thought; and he watched the birds flying home to their nests in the trees above him.

A blackbird flew quite close to him and whistled and chirped, "Goodnight, teddy bear."

"Goodnight, bird," said Teddy Robinson and waved an arm at him.

Then a snail came crawling past.

"Are you sleeping out tonight? That will be nice for you," he said. "Goodnight, teddy bear."

"Goodnight, snail," said Teddy Robinson, and he watched it crawl slowly away into the long grass.

She will come and fetch me soon, he thought. It must be getting quite late.

But Deborah didn't come and fetch him. Do you know why? She was fast asleep in bed!

This is what had happened. When she had run to see who was knocking at the front door, Deborah had found Uncle Michael standing on the doorstep. He had come in his new car, and he said there was just time to take her out for a ride if she came quickly, but she must hurry because he had to get into the town before teatime. There was only just time for Mummy to get Deborah's coat on and wave goodbye before they were off. They had come home ever so much later than they meant to because they had tea out in a shop, and then on the way home the new car had suddenly stopped and it took Uncle Michael a long time to find out what was wrong with it.

By the time they reached home Deborah was half-asleep, and Mummy had bundled her into bed before she had time to really wake up again and remember about Teddy Robinson still being in the garden.

He didn't know all this, of course, but he guessed something unusual must have happened to make Deborah forget about him.

Soon a little wind blew across the garden, and down fluttered some blossom from the almond-tree. It fell right in the middle of Teddy Robinson's tummy.

"Thank you," he said, "I like pink flowers for a blanket."

So the almond-tree shook its branches again, and more and more blossoms came tumbling down.

The garden tortoise came tramping slowly past.

"Hallo, teddy bear," he said. "Are you sleeping out? I hope you won't be cold. I felt a little breeze blowing up just now. I'm glad I've got my house with me."

*The garden tortoise
came tramping slowly past*

"But I have a fur coat," said Teddy Robinson, "and pink blossom for a blanket."

"So you have," said the tortoise. "That's lucky. Well, goodnight," and he drew his head into his shell and went to sleep close by.

The Next Door Kitten came padding softly through the grass and rubbed against him gently.

"You *are* out late," she said.

"Yes, I think I'm sleeping out tonight," said Teddy Robinson.

"Are you?" said the kitten. "You'll love that. I did it once. I'm going to do it a lot oftener when I'm older. Perhaps I'll stay out tonight."

But just then a window opened in the house next door and a voice called, "Puss! Puss! Puss! Come and have your fish! fish! fish!" and the kitten scampered off as fast as she could go.

Teddy Robinson heard the window shut down and then everything was quiet again.

The sky grew darker and darker blue, and soon the stars came out. Teddy Robinson lay and stared at them without blinking, and they twinkled and shone and winked at him as if they were surprised to see a teddy bear lying in the garden.

And after a while they began to sing to him, a very soft and sweet and far-away little song, to the tune of *Rock-a-Bye Baby*, and it went something like this:

> *"Rock-a-Bye Teddy, go to sleep soon.*
> *We will be watching, so will the moon.*
> *When you awake with dew on your paws*
> *Down will come Debbie and take you indoors."*

Teddy Robinson thought that was a lovely song, so when it was finished he sang one back to them. He sang it in a grunty voice because he was rather shy, and it went something like this:

> *"This is me*
> *under the tree,*
> *the bravest bear you ever did see.*

13

All alone
so brave I've grown,
I'm camping out on my very own."

The stars nodded and winked and twinkled to
show that they liked Teddy Robinson's song, and
then they sang *Rock-a-Bye Teddy* all over again, and
he stared and stared at them until he fell asleep.

Very early in the morning a blackbird whistled,
then another blackbird answered, and then all the
birds in the garden opened their beaks and twittered
and cheeped and sang. And Teddy Robinson
woke up.

One of the blackbirds hopped up with a worm in
his beak.

"Good morning, teddy bear," he said. "Would
you like a worm for your breakfast?"

"Oh, no, thank you," said Teddy Robinson. "I
don't usually bother about breakfast. Do eat it yourself."

"Thank you, I will," said the blackbird, and he
gobbled it up and hopped off to find some more.

Then the snail came slipping past.

"Good morning, teddy bear," he said. "Did you
sleep well?"

"Oh, yes, thank you," said Teddy Robinson.

14

"Would you like a worm for your breakfast?"

The Next Door Kitten came scampering up, purring.

"You lucky pur-r-son," she said as she rubbed against Teddy Robinson. "Your fur-r is damp but it was a pur-r-fect night for staying out. I didn't want to miss my fish supper last night, otherwise I'd have stayed with you. Pur-r-haps I will another night. Did you enjoy it?"

"Oh, yes," said Teddy Robinson. "You were quite right about sleeping out. It was lovely."

The tortoise poked his head out and blinked.

"Hallo," he said. "There's a lot of talking going on for so early in the morning. What is it all about? Oh,

She picked him up and hugged him.

good morning, bear. I'd forgotten you were here. I hope you had a comfortable night." And before Teddy Robinson could answer he had popped back inside his shell.

Then a moment later Teddy Robinson heard a little shuffling noise in the grass behind him, and there was Deborah out in the garden with bare feet, and in her pyjamas!

She picked him up and hugged him and kissed him and whispered to him very quietly, and then she ran through the wet grass and in at the kitchen door and up the stairs into her own room. A minute later she and Teddy Robinson were snuggled down in her warm little bed.

"You poor, poor boy," she whispered as she stroked his damp fur. "I never meant to leave you out all night. Oh, you poor, poor boy."

But Teddy Robinson whispered back, "I aren't a poor boy at all. I was camping out, and it was lovely." And then he tried to tell her all about the blackbird, and the snail, and the tortoise, and the kitten, and the stars. But because it was really so very early in the morning, and Deborah's bed was really so very warm and cosy, they both got drowsy; and before he had even got to the part about the stars singing their song to him both Teddy Robinson and Deborah were fast asleep.

And that is the end of the story about how
Teddy Robinson stayed out all night.

2

Teddy Robinson Goes
to the Toyshop

One day Teddy Robinson and Deborah were going with Mummy to a big toyshop. Deborah had ten shillings to spend. It had been sent to her at Christmas.

"You must help me choose my present, Teddy Robinson," said Deborah. "It will be nice for you to see all the toys."

"Yes," said Teddy Robinson. "You couldn't really manage without me. Shall I wear my best purple dress?"

"No," said Deborah, "your trousers will do. It isn't a party."

When they got to the toyshop there were so many things to look at that Deborah just couldn't make up her mind. Teddy Robinson got quite tired of being pushed up against the counter and squashed against ladies' shopping-baskets.

"Perhaps I'll have a glove-puppet," said Deborah.

"Then put me down for a bit," said Teddy Robinson. "I'm tired of being squashed, and I don't much care about glove-puppets anyway."

So Deborah sat Teddy Robinson down by a large dolls' house, and he sang a little song to himself while he was waiting. This is what he sang:

> *"See Saw,*
> *knock at the door,*
> *ask me in and shake my paw.*
> *How do you do? It's only me,*
> *it's half-past three,*
> *and I've come to tea."*

Teddy Robinson peeped through one of the upper windows of the dolls' house. A tiny little doll inside was sitting at a tiny little dressing-table. When she saw Teddy Robinson's big furry face looking in at the window she gave a tiny little scream. Then she said, in a tiny little, very cross voice:

"How dare you stare in at my window? How very rude of you!"

"I'm so sorry," said Teddy Robinson politely. "I'd no idea you were there. I was just looking to see if the windows were real or only painted on. I didn't

"*How dare you stare in at my window?*"

mean to look in your bedroom window."

The tiny little doll came over to the window of the dolls' house and looked out.

"That's the worst of living in a shop," she said. "Everybody comes poking about the house, and looking in at the windows, and asking how much you cost, and wanting to come inside and look round. Well, I'll tell you now – we cost a great deal of money, we're very dear indeed, and you *can't* come in and look round, so there!"

Then the tiny little doll made a rude face at Teddy Robinson, and pulled the tiny little muslin curtains across the tiny little windows so that he couldn't see inside any more.

"Dear me!" said Teddy Robinson to himself. "What a very cross lady! I'm sure *I* don't want to go in her house. I couldn't, anyway – I'm far too big. But it would have been politer if she'd asked me to, even though she could see I was too fat to get through the door."

Just then Deborah came over and picked Teddy Robinson up.

"I've decided I don't want a glove-puppet after all," she said, "so we're going to look at the dolls now."

So Deborah and Teddy Robinson and Mummy went to find the doll counter. On the way they passed dolls' prams, and scooters, and tricycles, and a little farther on they came to a toy motor-car with a big teddy bear sitting inside it.

"Oh, look!" said Deborah. "Isn't that lovely!"

"The dolls are over there," said Mummy, walking over to the counter.

"Listen, Teddy Robinson," said Deborah, "if I put you down here you can look at that bear in the car while I go and look at the dolls." And she put him down close to the car so that he wouldn't get walked on or knocked over, and ran off to join Mummy.

Teddy Robinson had a good look at the toy motor-car and the teddy bear sitting inside it. It was a beautiful car, very smart and shiny, and painted cream. The teddy bear inside it was very smart and shiny too. He had a blue satin bow at his neck, and pale golden fur which looked as though it had been brushed very carefully.

Teddy Robinson was surprised that he didn't seem at all excited to be sitting in such a beautiful car. He looked bored, and was leaning back against the driving-seat as if he couldn't even be bothered to sit up straight.

"Good afternoon," said Teddy Robinson. "I hope you don't mind me looking at your car?"

"Not at all, actually," said the bear in the car.

"Are you a shop bear?" asked Teddy Robinson.

"Yes, actually I am," said the bear.

"You've got a very fine car," said Teddy Robinson. "Are you going anywhere special in it?"

"No, actually I'm not at the moment," said the shop bear. "Don't lean against it, will you? It's a very expensive car, actually."

"No, I won't," said Teddy Robinson. "Why do you keep saying 'actually'?"

"Are you a shop bear?"

"It's only a way of making dull things sound more interesting," said the shop bear. "Anything else you want to know?"

"Yes," said Teddy Robinson. "Can you drive that car?"

"Actually, no," said the shop bear. Then, all of a sudden, he leaned over the driving-wheel and said in a quite different voice, "Look here, you're a nice chap – I don't mind your knowing. Don't tell, but it's all a pretend. This car doesn't belong to me at all, and I don't know how to drive it. They put me here just to make people look, and then they hope they'll buy the car."

"Fancy that!" said Teddy Robinson. "And I was thinking how lucky you were to have such a very fine car all of your own. You look so smart and handsome sitting inside it."

"Yes, I know," said the shop bear. "That's why they chose me to be the car salesman. But it's a dull life, really. If only I knew how to drive this car I'd drive right out of the shop one day and never come back."

"All the same," said Teddy Robinson, "it must be rather grand to be a car salesman."

"What are you?" asked the shop bear.

"Me? I'm a teddy bear. Don't I look like one?"

"Yes, of course," said the shop bear. "I meant, what is your job?"

Teddy Robinson had never been asked this question before, so he had to think hard for an answer.

"I suppose I'm what you'd call a Lady's Companion," he said. "I belong to that little girl over there. She isn't exactly a lady yet, but I expect she will be one day."

Just then Deborah ran back, so Teddy Robinson

had to say goodbye to the shop bear very quickly.

"You must come and see the dolls," said Deborah. "There aren't any nice ones for ten shillings, but some of them are simply beautiful just to look at."

She carried Teddy Robinson over to whcre Mummy was looking at a very large doll, dressed as a bride.

"Now just look at that one," said Deborah. "She's quite three times as big as you are, Teddy Robinson."

"And she can walk, and talk, and you can curl her hair," said the shop-lady who was standing by.

"She really is beautiful," said Mummy, looking at the price-ticket, "but we couldn't possibly buy her."

"Is she *very* dear, Mummy?" asked Deborah.

"Yes," said Mummy, "very dear indeed. She is five pounds."

"Dearer than me?" said Teddy Robinson.

"Oh, yes," said Deborah, "a lot dearer than you. She costs five whole pounds."

"Well," said Teddy Robinson, "if she costs five pounds I bet I cost a hundred pounds. Ask Mummy."

"Mummy," said Deborah, "how much did Teddy Robinson cost when he was new?"

"About twenty-nine and eleven, I think," said Mummy.

"Not as much as that doll?" said Deborah.

"Oh, no," said Mummy. "That doll is much dearer."

"Fancy that!" said Teddy Robinson to himself, and he felt half surprised and half cross to think he wasn't quite the dearest person in the whole world.

"I don't think it's much use our looking at dolls any more," said Mummy. "They're all so dear."

"Yes," said Deborah, "and I've just thought what I really would like to buy. Couldn't I have one of those dolls that are really hot-water bottles?"

"Why, yes," said Mummy. "What a good idea!"

So they all went along to the chemist's department, and there they saw three different kinds of hot-water-bottle dolls. There was a hot-water-bottle clown, and a hot-water-bottle Red-Riding-Hood, and a hot-water-bottle dog, bright blue with a pink bow.

Deborah picked up the blue dog.

"That's the one I want," she said. "Look, Teddy Robinson – do you like him?"

"Isn't he rather flat?" said Teddy Robinson.

"Yes, but he won't be when he's filled," said Deborah. "He's a dear – isn't he, Mummy?"

"Yes," said Mummy, "he really is."

"Everybody in this shop seems to be dear except me," said Teddy Robinson to himself. And he felt grumpy and sad; but nobody noticed him, because

"Isn't he rather flat?"

they were so busy looking at the blue dog, and paying for him, and watching him being put into a brown-paper bag.

All the way home Teddy Robinson went on feeling grumpy and sad. He thought about the doll dressed as a bride who was three times as big as he was.

"It isn't fair," he said to himself. "She didn't have to be three times as dear as me as well."

And he thought about the tiny little doll who

hadn't asked him into the dolls' house.

"She was a nasty, rude little doll," he said, "but she told me *she* was very dear too."

And he thought about the blue-dog hot-water bottle, who seemed to be coming home with them.

"Deborah and Mummy called *him* a dear, too. But I don't think he's a dear. I don't like him at all, and I hope he'll stay always inside that brown-paper bag."

But when they got home the blue dog was taken out of his brown-paper bag straight away. And when bedtime came something even worse happened. Teddy Robinson and Deborah got into bed as usual, and what should they find but the blue dog already there, lying right in the middle of the bed, and smiling up at them both, just as if he belonged there!

"*Look* at who's in our bed!" said Teddy Robinson to Deborah. "Make him get out."

"Of course he's in our bed," said Deborah. "That's what we bought him for, to keep us warm. Isn't he a dear?"

Teddy Robinson didn't say a word, he felt so cross. Deborah put her ear against his furry tummy.

"You're not *growling*, are you?" she said.

"Yes, I are!" shouted Teddy Robinson.

"But why?"

"Look at who's in our bed!"

"Because I don't like not being dear," said Teddy Robinson. "And if I aren't dear why do people always call me 'Dear Teddy Robinson' when they write to me?"

"But you *are* dear," said Deborah.

"No, I aren't," said Teddy Robinson; "and now I don't even *feel* dear any more. I just feel growly and grunty." And he told her all about what he had been thinking ever since they left the toyshop.

"But those are only dolls," said Deborah, "and this is only a hot-water bottle. You are my very dear

Teddy Robinson, and you're quite the dearest person in the whole world to me (not counting Daddy and Mummy and grown-ups, I mean)."

Teddy Robinson began to feel much better.

"Push the blue dog down by your feet, then," he said. "There isn't room for him up here."

So Deborah pushed the blue dog down, and Teddy Robinson cuddled beside her and thought how lucky he was not to be just a doll or a hot-water bottle.

Soon the blue dog made the bed so warm and cosy that Deborah fell asleep and Teddy Robinson began to get drowsy. He said, "Dear me, dear me," to himself, over and over again; and after a while he began to feel as if he loved everybody in the whole world. And soon his "Dear me's" turned into a sleepy little song which went like this:

> *"Dear me,*
> *dear me,*
> *how nice to be*
> *as dear*
> *a bear*
> *as dear old me.*
> *Dear you,*
> *dear him,*

dear them,
dear we,
dear every one,
and dear,
        dear
            me."

And then he fell fast asleep.

And that is the end of the story about how
Teddy Robinson went to the toyshop.

– 3 –

Teddy Robinson
Keeps House

One day Teddy Robinson sat on the kitchen table and watched everyone being very busy. Mummy was cutting bread, Deborah was putting some flowers in a vase of water, and Daddy was looking for a newspaper that had something in it that he specially wanted to read.

Teddy Robinson wished he could look busy too, but he couldn't think of anything to be looking busy about. He stared up at the ceiling. One or two flies were crawling about up there. Teddy Robinson began counting them; but every time he got as far as "Three" one of them would suddenly fly away and land somewhere quite different, so it was difficult to know if he had counted it before or not.

"What's the matter, Teddy Robinson?" said Deborah.

"Nothing's the matter," he said. "I'm busy. I'm

counting flies, but they keep flying away."

"Silly boy," said Deborah.

"No," said Mummy, "he's not silly at all. He's reminded me that I must get some fly-papers from the grocer today. We don't want flies crawling about in the kitchen."

Teddy Robinson felt rather pleased.

"I like being busy," he said. "What else can I do?"

Deborah put the vase of flowers on the table beside him.

"You can smell these flowers for me," she said.

Teddy Robinson leaned forward with his nose against the flowers and smelled them.

When Daddy had found his newspaper and gone off to work, Mummy put some slices of bread under the grill on the cooker.

"We will have some toast," she said.

"And you can watch it, Teddy Robinson," said Deborah.

Just then the front-door bell rang, and Mummy went out to see who it was. Teddy Robinson and Deborah could hear Andrew's voice. He was saying something about a picnic this afternoon, and could Deborah come too?

"Oh!" said Deborah. "I must go and find out about this!" And she ran out into the hall.

Teddy Robinson stayed sitting on the kitchen table watching the toast. He could hear the others talking by the front door, and then he heard Mummy saying, "I think I'd better come over and talk to your mummy about it now." And after that everything was quiet.

Teddy Robinson felt very happy to be so busy. He stared hard at the toast and sang to himself as he watched it turning from white to golden brown and then from golden brown to black.

In a minute he heard a little snuffling noise coming from the half-open back door. The Puppy from over the Road was peeping into the kitchen. When he saw Teddy Robinson sitting on the table he wagged his tail and smiled, with his pink tongue hanging out.

"What's cooking?" he said.

"Toast," said Teddy Robinson. "Won't you come in? There's nobody at home but me."

"Oh, no, I mustn't," said the puppy. "I'm not house-trained yet. Are you?"

"Oh, yes," said Teddy Robinson. "I can do quite a lot of useful things in the house."

He began thinking quickly of all the useful things he could do; then he said, "I can watch toast, keep people company, smell flowers, time eggs, count flies,

~ watching the toast ~

or sit on things to keep them from blowing away. Just at the minute I'm watching the toast."

"It makes an interesting smell, doesn't it?" said the puppy, sniffing the air.

"Yes," said Teddy Robinson. "It makes a lot of smoke too. That's what makes it so difficult to watch. You can't see the toast for the smoke, but I've managed to keep my eye on it nearly all the time. I've been making up a little song about it:

"I'm watching the toast.
I don't want to boast,
but I'm better than most
at watching the toast.

It can bake, it can boil,
it can smoke, it can roast,
but I stick to my post.
I'm watching the toast."

"Jolly good song," said the puppy. "But, you know, it's really awfully smoky in here. If you don't mind I think I'll just go and practise barking at a cat or two until you've finished. Are you sure you won't come out too? Come and have a breath of fresh air."

"No, no," said Teddy Robinson. "I'll stick to my post until the others come back."

And at that moment the others did come back.

"Oh, dear!" cried Mummy. "Whatever's happened? Oh, of course – it's the toast! I'd forgotten all about it."

"But I didn't," said Teddy Robinson proudly. "I've been watching it all the time."

"It was because Andrew came and asked us to a picnic this afternoon," said Deborah. "Would you like to come too?"

"I'd much rather stay at home and keep house," said Teddy Robinson. "I like being busy. Isn't there something I could do that would be useful?"

"Yes," said Mummy, when Deborah asked her. "The grocery order is coming this afternoon. If Teddy Robinson likes to stay he can look after it for us until we come home. We'll ask the man to leave it on the step and risk it."

So it was decided that Deborah and Mummy should go to the picnic and Teddy Robinson should stay at home and keep house.

When they were all ready to go, Mummy wrote a notice which said, PLEASE LEAVE GROCERIES ON THE STEP, and Deborah wrote underneath it, TEDDY ROBINSON WILL LOOK AFTER THEM. Then they put the notice on the back-door step, and Teddy Robinson sat on it so that it wouldn't blow away.

Deborah kissed him goodbye, and Mummy shut the back door behind him. Teddy Robinson felt very pleased and important, and thought how jolly it was to be so busy that he hadn't even time to go to a picnic.

"I don't care *how* many people come and ask me to picnics or parties today," he said to himself. "I just can't go to any of them. I'm far too busy."

Nobody did come to ask Teddy Robinson to a
party or a picnic, so after a while he settled down to
have a nice, quiet think. His think was all about how
lovely it would be if he had a little house all of his
own, where he could be as busy as he liked. He had a
picture in his mind of how he would open the door
to the milkman, and ask the baker to leave one small
brown, and invite people in for cups of tea. And he
would leave his Wellington boots just outside the

He had a picture in his mind

of how he would open the door to the milkman—

door (so as not to make the house muddy), and then say to people, "Excuse my boots, won't you?" So everybody would notice them, but nobody would think he was showing off about them. (Teddy Robinson hadn't got any Wellington boots, but he was always thinking how nice it would be if he had.)

He began singing to himself in a dreamy sort of way:

> "*Good morning, baker. One small brown.*
> *How much is that to pay?*
> *Good morning, milkman. Just one pint,*
> *and how's your horse today?*
>
> "*Good afternoon. How nice of you*
> *to come and visit me.*
> *Step right inside (excuse my boots).*
> *I'll make a pot of tea.*"

A blackbird flew down and perched on the garden fence. He whistled once or twice, looked at Teddy Robinson with his head on one side, and then flew away again.

A minute later the grocer's boy opened the side gate and came up to the back door. He had a great big cardboard box in his arms.

When he had read the notice he put the big box on the step. Then he picked Teddy Robinson up and sat him on top of it. He grinned at him, then he walked off, whistling loudly and banging the side gate behind him.

The blackbird flew down on to the fence again.

"Was that you whistling?" he asked.

"No," said Teddy Robinson, it was the grocer's boy."

"Did you hear me whistle just now?" asked the blackbird.

"Yes," said Teddy Robinson.

"I did it to see if you were real or not," said the blackbird. "You were sitting so still I thought you couldn't be, so I whistled to find out. Why didn't you answer me?"

"I can't whistle," said Teddy Robinson, "and, anyway, I was thinking."

"What's in that box?" asked the blackbird. "Any breadcrumbs?"

Just then there was a scrambling, scuffling noise, and the Puppy from over the Road came lolloping round the corner. The blackbird flew away.

"Hallo," said the puppy. "What are you doing here?"

"I'm guarding the groceries," said Teddy Robinson.

"I'm guarding the groceries"

"Well, I never!" said the puppy. "You were making toast last time I saw you. You do work hard. Do you have to make beds as well?"

"No," said Teddy Robinson, "I couldn't make beds. I haven't got a hammer and nails. But I am very busy today."

"Why don't they take the groceries in?" asked the puppy.

"They've gone to a picnic," said Teddy Robinson. "I stayed behind to keep house. They decided to let the boy leave the groceries on the step and risk it."

"What's 'risk-it'?" said the puppy.

"I don't know," said Teddy Robinson, "but I like saying it, because it goes so nicely with biscuit."

"Got any biscuits in there?" asked the puppy, sniffing round the box.

"I'm not sure," said Teddy Robinson, "but you mustn't put your nose in the box."

"I was only sniffing," said the puppy.

"You mustn't sniff either," said Teddy Robinson. "It's a bad habit."

"What's 'habit'?" said the puppy.

"I don't know," said Teddy Robinson. "But it goes very nicely with rabbit."

Suddenly the back door opened behind him. The puppy scuttled away, and Teddy Robinson found that Deborah and Mummy had come home again.

"You did keep house well," said Mummy, as she carried him into the kitchen with the box of groceries.

"Don't you think he ought to have a present," said Deborah, "for being so good at housekeeping?"

"He really ought to have a house of his own," said Mummy. "Look – what about this?" She pointed to the big box. "You could make him a nice house out of that when it's empty. I'll help you to cut the windows out."

"Oh, *yes*," said Deborah, "that is exactly what he wants."

So after tea Deborah and Mummy got busy making a beautiful little house for Teddy Robinson. They made a door and two windows (one at the front and one at the back) and painted them green. Then Deborah made a hole in the lid of the box and stuck a cardboard chimney in it. Mummy painted a rambler-rose climbing up the wall. It looked very pretty.

"What would you like to call your house?" said Deborah. "Do you think Rose Cottage would be a nice name?"

"I'd rather it had my own name on it," said Teddy Robinson.

So Deborah painted TEDDY ROBINSON'S HOUSE over the door, and then it was all ready.

The next day Teddy Robinson's house was put out in the garden in the sunshine. He chose to have it close to the flower-bed at the edge of the lawn, and all day long he sat inside and waited for people to call on him. Deborah came to see him quite often, and every time she looked in at the window and said, "What are you doing now, Teddy Robinson?" he would say, "I'm just thinking about what to have for dinner," or "I'm just having a rest before getting tea."

"I never knew there was a house there"

The Puppy from over the Road came and called on him too. He sniffed at Teddy Robinson through the open window and admired him more than ever now that he had a house of his own.

And the garden tortoise came tramping out of the flower-bed and looked up at the house, saying, "Well, well, I never knew there was a house there!"

Then the Next Door Kitten came walking round on tiptoe. At first she didn't quite believe it was real. She was sniffing at the rambler-rose painted on the wall when Teddy Robinson looked out of the window and said, "Good afternoon."

The kitten purred with pleasure at seeing him.

"What a purr-r-rfect little house!" she said. "Is it really yours? You *are* a lucky purr-r-rson."

Teddy Robinson nodded and smiled at her from the window.

"Yes," he said, "it's my very own house. Aren't I lucky? It's just what I've always wanted – a little place all of my own."

And that is the end of the story about how
Teddy Robinson kept house.

– 4 –

Teddy Robinson Has a Birthday Party

O ne day Teddy Robinson said to Deborah, "You know, I've lived with you for years and years and years, and yet I've never had a birthday. Why haven't I?"

"I suppose it's because you came at Christmas," said Deborah, "so we've never thought about it. Would you like to have a birthday?"

"Oh, yes, please," said Teddy Robinson, "if you can spare one. And can I have a party?"

"Yes, I think it's a lovely idea," said Deborah. "When would you like your birthday to be?"

"Today?" said Teddy Robinson.

"No, not today," said Deborah. "There wouldn't be time to get a party ready. I shall have to ask Mummy about it. Besides, I haven't got a present for you."

"Tomorrow, then," said Teddy Robinson.

"All right," said Deborah. "We'll make it tomorrow. How old would you like to be?"

"A hundred," said Teddy Robinson.

"Don't be silly," said Deborah. "You can't be a hundred."

"Why not? I've been here about a hundred years, haven't I?"

"No, of course you haven't," said Deborah. "I know it seems a long while, but it's not as long as all that. I think you're about three or four. I'll ask Mummy."

Mummy thought it would be a good idea for Teddy Robinson to have a party.

"You can ask Philip and Mary-Anne to tea," she said, "and I'll make some things for you to eat. Would Teddy Robinson like a birthday cake?"

"Oh, *yes*," said Deborah, "with candles on. But how old is he?"

"I think he's three really," said Mummy, "but I'm afraid he'll have to be one tomorrow, because there's only one cake candle left in the box."

So everybody started getting ready for Teddy Robinson's birthday party.

Deborah bought him a little trumpet for three-pence and wrapped it up in pink tissue paper. Then she made a paper crown for him to wear on his head

She made a paper crown for him to wear.

(because he was going to be the birthday king). Mummy made the cake, and iced it, and wrote TEDDY on top with tiny silver balls. Then she made a lot of very small jellies in egg-cups. And Teddy Robinson sat and sang to himself all day long, and felt very proud and important, because he was going to have a birthday all of his own.

It was beautifully sunny the next day, so Deborah and Teddy Robinson decided they would have the party in the garden.

"We will have the little nursery-table under the almond-tree," said Deborah, "and you shall sit at the head, Teddy Robinson, and wear your purple dress and the birthday crown."

"Yes," he said, "that will be lovely."

"Now I must find something for us all to sit on,"

said Deborah. "I think my own little chair and stool will do for Mary-Anne and me, and the dolls will have to sit on the benches. Philip can have the toy-box turned upside down."

"And will there be three chairs for me?" asked Teddy Robinson.

"No, not *three*," said Deborah. "Why ever should you want three?"

"But don't they always have three chairs for somebody special?"

"Oh, you mean three *cheers*," said Deborah. "That means three hoorays."

"Oh," said Teddy Robinson; "then can I have three hoorays if I can't have three chairs?"

"Yes, I expect so," said Deborah. "Now, don't interrupt me, because I want to get everything ready."

So Teddy Robinson sat and watched Deborah putting the chairs and benches out, and began singing his three hoorays, because he was so happy and excited.

> *"Hooray, hooray, hooray,*
> *my birthday party's today.*
> *You can come to tea*
> *at half-past three,*
> *and stay for ever, hooray."*

"Oh, don't say that," said Deborah. "It will all have to be cleared away and washed up afterwards, so we can't have people staying for ever."

"All right, then," said Teddy Robinson:

> *"Hooray, hooray, hooray,*
> *my birthday party's today.*
> *You can come to tea*
> *at half-past three,*
> *and stay until we tell you to go, unless*
> *somebody's fetching you."*

"Is that better?"

"Yes," said Deborah, but she wasn't really listening, because she was so busy thinking about where everybody was going to sit, and what she should use for a tablecloth, and whether there would be enough cups and saucers.

At half-past three the visitors arrived. The dolls were already sitting in their places, admiring the birthday cake with its one candle, and the little jellies, and the chocolate biscuits, and the piles of tiny sandwiches that Mummy had made.

And Teddy Robinson, wearing his best purple dress and his crown, was sitting on a high stool at the head of the table, and feeling like the King of all teddy bears.

admiring the birthday cake

"You do look grand," said Philip. "May I sit beside you?"

"Oh, yes," said Teddy Robinson, and felt very pleased at being asked. Philip gave him a small tin cow and some dolly mixture in a matchbox for his present.

"Oh, thank you," said Teddy Robinson. "I love cows, and Deborah loves dolly mixture. That *is* a good present."

Mary-Anne had brought Jacqueline with her. Jacqueline was her beautiful doll, who wore a pink silk dress and a frilly bonnet to match. Teddy Robinson was surprised to see that Jacqueline's eyes were shut, although she wasn't lying down.

Mary-Anne said, "Many happy returns of the day, Teddy Robinson. This is Jacqueline. Her eyes are

Nobody minded her eyes being shut.

shut, because she's rather tired today." ("They're stuck, really," she whispered to Deborah.) "But she is *so* looking forward to the party."

Jacqueline had such a beautiful smile that nobody minded her eyes being shut, and Teddy Robinson was very pleased when she was put to sit on his other side at the table.

"And this is Jacqueline's present to you," said Mary-Anne, and she put a little parcel down on the table in front of him. Inside was a beautiful little paper umbrella. It was red with a yellow frill all round the outside edge.

Teddy Robinson was very pleased indeed. "It's just what I was wanting," he said. "Can I have it up now?"

"Yes," said Deborah, "it can be a sunshade today."

And she opened it up for him. With a sunshade as well as a crown, Teddy Robinson felt grander than ever.

They had a lovely tea. Deborah poured the milk into the dolls' cups and saucers while Mary-Anne handed round the sandwiches, and Philip made everybody laugh by telling them funny stories.

Every time Teddy Robinson laughed, he fell sideways against Philip, and his crown went over one eye, and this made everyone laugh more than ever.

"Don't make him so excited," said Deborah. "You're making him behave badly." But Teddy Robinson just got jollier and jollier. He was having a

every time he laughed he fell sideways

wonderful time. He began singing:

> *"Ding, dong,*
> *this is the song*
> *I'll sing at my birthday tea.*
> *I'm glad you came,*
> *but all the same,*
> *the party's really for me . . ."*

"Teddy Robinson!" said Deborah. "What a rude thing to sing to your visitors!"

"Oh, sorry!" said he. "I didn't really mean that. All right, I won't sing. I'll ask you a riddle instead. When is a bear bare?"

"What does it mean?" asked the dolls. "It doesn't make sense."

"When he's got no fur on!" said Teddy Robinson, and laughed until he fell sideways again. As nobody else understood the riddle they didn't think it was funny, but they laughed like anything when Teddy Robinson fell sideways, because his crown fell over his eyes again, and the umbrella came down on top of his head.

When it was time for the birthday cake everyone sang *Happy Birthday to You*, and just for a minute Teddy Robinson forgot to feel jolly, and felt rather shy instead. But as soon as they had finished he got jollier than ever.

"I feel just like standing on my head," he said.

"Go on, then," said Philip. "I'll help you."

"No, don't," said Deborah. But Teddy Robinson was already standing on his head in the middle of the table with Philip holding on to him.

"I feel just like standing on my head."

"Well done!" shouted Philip, as Teddy Robinson's fat, furry legs wobbled in the air. All the dolls laughed except Jacqueline, who couldn't see, because her eyes were shut, but she went on smiling all the time.

"Now I'll go head-over-heels!" said Teddy Robinson, and over he went.

"Mind the biscuits!" cried Mary-Anne, and took

them away just in time as Teddy Robinson came down with a bump that clattered all the cups and saucers. Everybody laughed and clapped except Deborah, who didn't like to see Teddy Robinson getting so rough.

"Do be careful!" she said. "Philip, put him back on his stool. Teddy Robinson, you really mustn't behave like that."

"All right, I won't do it again," said Teddy Robinson. "I'll sing about it instead." And then he began singing in a silly, squeaky little voice:

> *"The Birthday Bear,*
> *the Birthday Bear*
> *stood on his head*
> *with his legs in the air,*
> *and everyone laughed*
> *as the Bear with the crown*
> *went head-over-heels*
> *like a circus clown,*
> *and they laughed and laughed*
> *till he tumbled down.*
> *Hooray for the Birthday Bear!"*

He was so pleased with himself when he had sung this little song that he fell over backwards and disappeared out of sight under the table. Deborah pulled him out and brushed the cake-crumbs and dry leaves and little bits of jelly off his fur, then she sat him up at the table again.

"Don't be so silly," she said. "What ever will your visitors think?"

"They'll think I'm jolly funny," said Teddy Robinson, "though as a matter of fact, I didn't mean to fall over at all that time. I just leaned back, and there was nothing behind me, so I fell through it." Then he began singing again in the silly squeaky voice:

> *"Nothing was there,*
> *so the Birthday Bear*
> *leaned back, and fell right through it.*
> *Down with a smack*
> *he fell on his back!*
> *Wasn't he clever to do it?"*

Everybody started laughing again at this, so Teddy Robinson thought he would be funnier than ever. He leaned sideways against Jacqueline, so hard that she fell sideways against the doll next to her; and then they all went down like a lot of ninepins, and fell squeaking and giggling under the table.

Ex-and-shoff.

"I'm so sorry," said Deborah to Mary-Anne. "I'm afraid he's a little ex-and-shoff."

"What is that?" asked Mary-Anne.

"Excited and showing off," whispered Deborah, "but I don't want him to hear."

"I *did* hear!" shouted Teddy Robinson from under the table. "Ex-and-shoff yourself!"

Mary-Anne and Deborah took no notice of this, but Philip laughed. Deborah said, "I think it's your fault, Philip, that he's behaving so badly. You always laugh when he says something rude."

They picked up all the dolls from under the table, and when at last they were all sitting in their places again Deborah began handing round the chocolate biscuits. She put one on each plate, and each doll said "Thank you," but when she came to Teddy Robinson's place and looked up to speak to him she found she was looking at the back of his head.

"Teddy Robinson!" she said. "How dare you sit with your back to the table!"

"I'm not," said Teddy Robinson in a funny laughing voice.

"You are. Now, don't be so rude and silly. Turn round the other way, and put your feet under the table."

"My feet *are* under the table," said Teddy

"How dare you sit with your back to the table!"

Robinson, laughing more than ever.

Deborah lifted the cloth, and was very surprised to see that Teddy Robinson was quite right. His feet *were* under the table, but his face was still looking the other way, because his head was twisted right round from back to front.

"You *silly* boy!" she said, as she twisted it round again. "You deserve to get it stuck that way. Now, do behave yourself. You're not being funny at all."

"*We* think he is very funny," said one of the dolls politely.

"Thank you," said Teddy Robinson, and he bowed so low that this time he fell with his nose in the jam, and his crown fell off into the jellies.

"Now," said Deborah, when they had all finished laughing, "I think we'd better eat up the rest of the food before any more of it gets spilt or sat on."

So they finished up all the chocolate biscuits, and all the little jellies, and went on eating until there was nothing left but one tiny sandwich which nobody had any room for. Then, as it was time for the party to end, Philip said:

"Let's have three cheers for Teddy Robinson!"

Everyone shouted "Hip-Hip-Hooray" three times over; and Teddy Robinson bowed again (but this time he didn't fall over) and said, "Thank you for having me," because by now he was getting a bit muddled and had forgotten that it was his own party that he was enjoying so much.

And then everybody said "Goodbye," and "Thank you for having me," and "Thank you for coming," and "Wasn't it a lovely party," and Philip and Mary-Anne and Jacqueline went home, and the dolls went back to the toy-cupboard, and the party was really over.

Teddy Robinson, tired and happy, lay on the grass beside his birthday crown and umbrella. Deborah picked him up and carried him into the house.

"Well, Teddy Robinson," she said, "I hope you enjoyed your birthday party?"

"Oh, yes! It was the best one I ever had."

"It's a pity you didn't behave a *little* bit better," said Deborah. "You're getting a big boy now."

"Yes, but, after all, I was only *one* today, wasn't I?"

"Of *course* you were; I quite forgot!" said Deborah, and kissed him on the end of his nose.

And that is the end of the story about
Teddy Robinson's birthday party.

– 5 –

Teddy Robinson Goes to the Dancing-Class

One Saturday morning Teddy Robinson saw that Deborah was putting on her best dress.

"Where are we going?" he said.

"To a dancing-class," said Deborah, "to learn to dance. Won't it be fun?"

"What, me?"

"Yes, you can come too. Will you like that?"

"I don't think I'd better dance," said Teddy Robinson, "but I shall like to come and watch."

So he waited while Deborah put on her best socks and shoes, and had a red ribbon tied in her hair; then Deborah brushed his fur with the dolls' hair brush, and they were all ready to go.

"Oh, my shoes!" said Deborah. "Where are they?"

"On your feet," said Teddy Robinson, surprised.

"No, not these shoes," said Deborah. "I meant my dancing-shoes. I've got some new ones. They're very special – pink, with ribbons to keep them on."

"Well I never!" said Teddy Robinson. "You *have* gone grand and grown-up. Fancy having special shoes to dance in!"

Mummy had the new shoes all ready in a bag.

"You can see them when we get there," she said.

So they all set off, Mummy carrying the new shoes, Deborah hopping and skipping all the way, and Teddy Robinson singing to himself as he bounced up and down in her arms:

> *"Hoppity-skippity,*
> *rin-tin-tin –*
> *special shoes for dancing in,*
> *pink, with ribbons –*
> *well, fancy that!*
> *I'd dance myself if I wasn't so fat."*

When they got there Teddy Robinson stopped singing, and Deborah stopped hopping and skipping, and they followed Mummy into the cloakroom. Deborah changed into the new shoes, and had her hair brushed all over again; then they all went into the big hall.

Mary Jane was there, in a pale yellow dress with a frilly petticoat; and Caroline, with pink ribbons to match her party frock; and there was Andrew, in blue corduroy velvet trousers and shoes with silver buckles on them.

"Hallo, Teddy Robinson," said Andrew. "Have you come to dance?"

"Not today," said Teddy Robinson. "I didn't bring my shoes."

"He is going to watch," said Deborah, and she put him down on an empty chair in the front row. Then she ran off to talk to Mary Jane and Caroline.

All the mothers and aunties and nurses who had come to watch the class were chatting together in the rows of chairs behind Teddy Robinson, and on the chair next to him sat a large walkie-talkie doll, wearing a pink frilled dress with a ribbon sash. She was sitting up very straight, smiling and staring in front of her.

Teddy Robinson wondered whether to speak to her, but just then a lady came in and sat down at the piano, and a moment later the teacher, whose name was Miss Silver, came into the hall.

Teddy Robinson decided he had better not start talking now, as the class was about to begin. Instead he listened to all the mothers and aunties and nurses, who had all begun talking to the children at once, in busy, whispering voices.

"Stand up nicely, point your toes."

"Here's your hankie, blow your nose."

"Don't be shy now, do your best. Make it up and follow the rest."

"Where's your hankie? Did you blow?"

"There's the music. Off you go!"

Then the children all ran into the middle of the floor, and the dancing-class began.

Teddy Robinson, sitting tidily on his chair in the front row, thought how jolly it was to be one of the grown-ups who had come to watch, and how lucky he was to belong to the nicest little girl in the class.

"How pretty she looks in her new pink shoes and her red ribbon," he said to himself. "And how well she can dance already! She is doing it quite differently from all the others. When they are doing *hop, one-two-three* she is doing *one-two-three, hop, hop, hop*, and it looks so much jollier that way. She is the only one able to do it right. None of the others can keep up with her."

He smiled proudly as Deborah went dancing past, her eyes shining, her red ribbon flying.

A lady in the row behind whispered to someone else, "Who is that little girl with the red ribbon, the one who hops three times instead of once?"

The other lady whispered back, "I don't know.

She is new, you can see that – but isn't she enjoying herself? That's her teddy bear on the chair in front."

Teddy Robinson pretended he wasn't listening and hummed softly to himself in time to the music. He was pleased that other people had noticed Deborah too. He looked sideways at the walkie-talkie doll. She was still smiling, and watching the dancing carefully. Teddy Robinson was glad to think that she too was admiring Deborah.

When the music stopped and the children paused for breath Teddy Robinson turned to her.

"Aren't you dancing?" he asked.

"Aren't you dancing?"

"No," said the doll; "I walk and talk, but I don't dance. I've come to watch."

"I've come to watch too," said Teddy Robinson.

"I suppose you don't dance either?" said the doll, looking at Teddy Robinson's fat tummy.

"No, I sing," said Teddy Robinson.

"Ah, yes," said the doll, "you have the figure for it."

The children began dancing again, and the lady at the piano played such hoppity-skippity music that Teddy Robinson couldn't help joining in with a little song, very quietly to himself:

> *"Hoppity-skippity, one-two-three,*
> *The bestest dancer belongs to me.*
> *Oh, what a fortunate bear I be!*
> *Hoppity-skippity, one-two-three."*

The walkie-talkie doll turned to Teddy Robinson.

"How beautifully she dances!" she said. "I'm not surprised so many people have come to watch her."

"Thank you," said Teddy Robinson, bowing slightly, and feeling very proud. "Yes, she does dance well and this is her first lesson."

"Oh, no, it's not," said the doll. "I bring her every Saturday. She's had quite a number of lessons already."

"I beg your pardon," said Teddy Robinson. "Who are we talking about?"

"My little girl, Mary, of course," said the doll, "the one with the yellow curls."

"Oh," said Teddy Robinson, "I thought we were talking about my little girl, Deborah, the one with the red ribbon."

The doll didn't seem to hear. She was staring at the children with a fixed smile. Miss Silver was arranging them in two rows, the girls on one side, the boys on the other.

Teddy Robinson and the walkie-talkie doll both kept their eyes fixed on the girls' row.

"She looks so pretty, doesn't she?" said the doll. "I do admire her dress, don't you?"

"Yes," said Teddy Robinson, looking at Deborah.

"That pale blue suits her so well," said the doll.

"Thank you," said Teddy Robinson, "I'm glad you like it; but it isn't pale blue – it's white."

"Oh no, it's pale blue," said the doll. "I helped her mother to choose it myself."

Teddy Robinson looked puzzled.

"Are you talking about the little girl with the red hair-ribbon?" he asked.

"No, of course not," said the doll. "Why should I be? I'm talking about Mary."

"Whoever is Mary?" said Teddy Robinson.

"The little girl we have all come to watch," said the doll. "*My* little girl. We've been talking about her all the time."

"*I* haven't," said Teddy Robinson. "I've been talking about Deborah."

"Deborah?" said the doll. "Whoever is Deborah?"

"What a silly creature this doll is!" said Teddy Robinson to himself. "She doesn't seem able to keep her mind on the class at all." And he decided not to bother about talking to her any more. Instead he listened to Miss Silver, who was teaching the boys and girls how to bow and curtsy to each other.

"I must watch this carefully," said Teddy Robinson to himself. "I should like to know how to bow properly – it might come in handy at any time. I might be asked to tea at Buckingham Palace or happen to meet the Queen out shopping one day, and I should look very silly if I didn't know how to make my bow properly."

As the boys all bowed from the waist Teddy Robinson leaned forward on his chair.

"Lower!" cried Miss Silver.

The boys all bowed lower, and Teddy Robinson leaned forward as far as he could; but he went just a little too far, and a moment later he fell head over heels on to the floor. Luckily, no one knew he had been practising his bow, they just thought he had toppled off his chair by mistake, as anyone might – so they took no notice of him.

Then it was the girls' turn to curtsy. The line of little girls wobbled and wavered, and Deborah wobbled so much that she too fell on the floor. But after three tries she did manage to curtsy without falling over, and Teddy Robinson was very proud of her.

"Never mind," said Miss Silver, as she said good-bye to them at the end of the class. "You did very well for a first time. You can't expect to learn to dance in one lesson. But you did enjoy it, didn't you?"

"Oh, yes!" said Deborah. "It was lovely."

"What did she mean?" said Teddy Robinson, as soon as they were outside. "I thought you danced better than anybody."

"Oh, no," said Deborah. "I think I was doing it all wrong, but it *was* fun. I'm glad we're going again next Saturday."

"Well I never!" said Teddy Robinson. "I quite thought you were the only one doing it right. Never mind. Did you see when I fell off the chair? That was me trying to bow. I don't think I did it very well either."

"You did very well for a first time too," said

Deborah. "You can't expect to learn to bow in one lesson. We must practise together at home, though. You can learn to bow to me while I practise doing my curtsy."

"That will be very nice," said Teddy Robinson. "Then next time we shan't both end up on the floor."

That night Teddy Robinson had a most Beautiful Dream. He dreamt he was in a very large theatre, with red velvet curtains, tied with large golden tassels, on each side of the stage.

Every seat in the theatre was full; Teddy Robinson himself was sitting in the middle of the front row, and all the people were watching Deborah, who was dancing all alone on the stage in her new pink dancing-shoes. She was dressed like a princess, in a frilly white dress with a red sash, and she had a silver crown on her head.

The orchestra was playing sweetly, and Deborah was dancing so beautifully that soon everyone was whispering and asking who she was.

Teddy Robinson heard someone behind him saying, "She belongs to that handsome bear in the front row, the one in the velvet suit and lace collar."

Teddy Robinson looked round, but couldn't see any bear in a velvet suit and lace collar. Then he

"She belongs to that handsome bear in the front row."

looked down and saw that instead of his ordinary trousers he was wearing a suit of beautiful blue velvet, with a large lace collar fastened at the neck with a silver pin. And in his lap was a bunch of roses tied with silver ribbon.

"Goodness gracious, they must have meant me!" he thought, and felt his fur tingling with pleasure and excitement.

As the music finished and Deborah came to the front of the stage to curtsy, Teddy Robinson felt

He felt himself floating through the air

himself floating through the air with his bunch of roses, and a moment later he landed lightly on the stage beside her. A murmur went up from the audience, "Ah, here is Teddy Robinson himself!"

Folding one paw neatly across his tummy, he bowed low to Deborah. Then, as she took the roses from him and they both bowed and curtsyed again, everyone in the theatre clapped so loudly that Teddy Robinson woke up and found he was in bed beside Deborah.

At first he was so surprised that he could hardly believe he was really at home in bed, but just then

bowed and curtsyed together

Deborah woke up too. She rolled over, smiling, with her eyes shut, and said, "Oh, Teddy Robinson, I've just had such a Beautiful Dream! I must tell you all about it."

So she did. And the funny thing was that Deborah had dreamt exactly the same dream as Teddy Robinson. She remembered every bit of it.

And that is the end of the story about
how Teddy Robinson went to the dancing-class.

6

Teddy Robinson and the Teddy-Bear Brooch

One day a letter came for Deborah and Teddy Robinson. It was from Auntie Sue, and it said:

DEAR DEBORAH AND TEDDY ROBINSON,
   Please tell Mummy I shall be coming to tea with you all tomorrow. I hope you will like the little brooch.

And pinned to a card inside the letter was a dear little teddy-bear brooch. It was pink with silver eyes, and Deborah thought it was very beautiful. She gave the letter to Mummy to read and pinned the brooch on the front of her dress.

"Wasn't there anything for me?" asked Teddy Robinson. Deborah looked inside the envelope again.

"No," she said, "there's nothing else."

"Oh," said Teddy Robinson. "Then can I have

the envelope? It will make me a soldier's hat."

So Deborah put the envelope on his head. Then Teddy Robinson said, "Fetch me the wooden horse, please. It's time I went on duty. I'm going to guard the palace."

So Deborah fetched the wooden horse.

"And I want a sentry-box, please," said Teddy Robinson.

"I haven't got a sentry-box," said Deborah. "Will the toy-box do?"

"Yes, if you stand it up on end," said Teddy Robinson.

So Deborah emptied the toy-box and stood it up on end. Then she put the wooden horse inside, and Teddy Robinson sat on its back with the envelope on his head. He didn't really feel like playing soldiers at all, but he wanted to sit somewhere quietly and not be talked to for a while.

"Do you *really* like it in there?" asked Deborah, peeping in at him.

"Yes, thank you," said Teddy Robinson, "but you mustn't talk to me. I'm on duty."

So Deborah went off to play by herself, and Teddy Robinson sat on the wooden horse and began thinking about why he was feeling so quiet. He knew it was something to do with

"Do you really _like_ it in there?"

the teddy-bear brooch.

He began mumbling to himself in a gentle, grumbling growl:

> "Fancy *her sending a brooch with a bear!*
> *It isn't polite and it isn't fair.*
> *There's a bear here already*
> *who lives in the house.*
> *Why* couldn't *she send her a brooch*
>   *with a mouse?*
> *Or a brooch with a dog?*
> *Or a brooch with a cat?*
> *Nobody'd* ever *feel hurt at that.*
> *But a brooch with a bear*
> *isn't fair*
> *on the bear*
> *who lives in the house,*
> *and who's* always *been there.*"

Teddy Robinson went on mumbling to himself and getting more and more grumbly and growly. He was feeling very cross with Auntie Sue, so he said all the nasty things he could think of, for quite a long while. Then he ended up by saying:

> "*When* she *gets a present I only hope*
> "*that all* she *gets is an envelope.*"

"Fancy her sending a brooch with a bear!"

After that he began to feel quite sorry for Auntie Sue, and much better himself.

He heard Mummy come out into the garden and say to Deborah, "Hallo! Why ever have you emptied the toy-box and stood it up on end like that?"

And he heard Deborah say, "Hush! Teddy Robinson's inside. He says he's guarding the palace, but I think he's sad about something."

"Oh, well," said Mummy, "bring him with you. I

was going to ask if you would like to help make a fruit jelly for Auntie Sue tomorrow."

"Oh, yes," said Deborah. "Teddy Robinson can sit on the kitchen table and watch. He always likes that."

She bent down and peeped inside the toy-box.

"Have you finished guarding the palace yet, Teddy Robinson?"

"Yes, I'm just coming off duty this minute," said Teddy Robinson. "Help me down."

Deborah helped him down, and together they went into the kitchen. Mummy had poured some pink jelly into a bowl, and she gave Deborah some cherries and slices of banana on a plate.

"Drop them into the jelly, one at a time," said Mummy. "It's still rather soft and runny, but tomorrow it will be set beautifully, with the fruit inside it."

So Deborah knelt on a chair and dropped the pieces of fruit carefully into the bowl, and Teddy Robinson sat on the kitchen table and said "Plop" every time she dropped a cherry in, and "Bang" every time she dropped a slice of banana in. He always liked helping when Deborah was working with Mummy in the kitchen.

Every time Deborah leaned forward to look in the bowl, Teddy Robinson saw the teddy-bear brooch on her dress, its silver eyes shining and winking in the sunlight. He tried not to look, because he didn't want to feel cross again; but it was so pretty it was difficult not to notice it.

And then Teddy Robinson saw that the pin of the brooch had come undone, and every time Deborah moved it was sliding a little way farther out of her dress. He held his breath, waiting to see what would happen, and a moment later it slipped out and fell with a gentle *plop* right into the middle of the jelly-bowl!

Deborah was saying something to Mummy at the minute, so she did not notice. Teddy Robinson wondered if he ought to tell her, but it seemed a pity to remind her about it.

"After all, she's still got me," he said to himself. "She didn't really need another teddy bear."

He looked down into the bowl, but there was no sign of the teddy-bear brooch. If it was there it was well hidden among all the cherries and banana slices. Teddy Robinson was glad to think it had gone.

Deborah dropped the last slice of banana into the bowl.

"There," she said, "it's all finished. You forgot to say 'Bang', Teddy Robinson."

"Bang," said Teddy Robinson. "Do you feel as if

He looked down into the bowl

you'd lost something?"

"No," said Deborah. "Do you?"

"No," said Teddy Robinson. "At least, if I have I'm glad I've lost it."

"You *are* a funny boy," said Deborah. "I don't know what you're talking about."

Teddy Robinson began to feel very jolly now that the teddy-bear brooch had gone. He kept singing funny little songs, and asking Deborah silly riddles, and making her laugh, so that it wasn't until after tea that she suddenly noticed she had lost it.

"Oh dear! Wherever can it be?" she said. "It must have fallen off while we were playing. Help me look for it, Teddy Robinson."

They couldn't find it anywhere.

So Teddy Robinson and Deborah looked under chairs and under tables and all through the toy-cupboard, but, of course, they couldn't find it anywhere.

Teddy Robinson began to sing:

> *"Oh, where, oh, where*
> *is the Broochy Bear?*
> *First look here,*
> *and then look there.*
> *I can't see him anywhere.*
> *He's lost! He's lost! The Broochy Bear!"*

"You sound as if you're glad he's lost," said Deborah. "Why are you so jolly?"

"Because I'm jolly sorry," said Teddy Robinson.

"Oh, don't be so silly," said Deborah. "Let's go and ask Mummy."

But Mummy hadn't seen the teddy-bear brooch anywhere either. "He must be somewhere about," she said. "You'll just have to go on looking."

"But we've looked everywhere – haven't we, Teddy Robinson?"

"Well, we haven't looked everywhere," he said, "because we haven't looked on top of the roof, or under the floor, or up the chimney, but we did look in quite a lot of places."

"But I haven't been on top of the roof, or under the floor, or up the chimney," said Deborah.

"No," said Teddy Robinson, "but you haven't been in the jelly either."

"What are you talking about?" said Deborah. "And why are you so jolly? I don't see anything to feel so happy about."

The next day Auntie Sue came at teatime, as she had promised. She was very pleased to see everybody, and because she was his friend as well, Teddy Robinson was allowed to sit up at the table. He had a chair with three cushions on it, so he was high enough to have quite a nice view of everything.

There were sandwiches and cakes and chocolate biscuits, and in the middle of the table was the fruit jelly. It had set beautifully, and Mummy had turned it out on to a glass dish.

Deborah pointed it out to Auntie Sue.

"Teddy Robinson and I helped to make that," she said.

"Did you really?" said Auntie Sue. "How very clever of you both!"

She turned to smile at them, and then she said:

"Why isn't Teddy Robinson wearing his brooch? Didn't he like it?"

"Oh!" said Deborah. "Was it for him? How dreadful! I thought it was for me, and I pinned it on the front of my dress, and now I've lost it. I can't think where it is."

"It's sure to turn up soon," said Mummy. "We know it's somewhere in the house." Then she and Auntie Sue started talking together about grown-up things.

"Never mind, Teddy Robinson," whispered Deborah. "I'm sure we shall find him again soon."

"The trouble is he mayn't be there any more to find," said Teddy Robinson.

"Where?" asked Deborah.

"Where he was yesterday when we couldn't find him," said Teddy Robinson. "I'm afraid he may have melted."

"What ever do you mean?" said Deborah. "Do you know where he is? If you do I wish you'd tell me."

"Well," said Teddy Robinson, "think of something round and pink, with a lot of banana in it, that's on the table, and when you've guessed what I mean I'll tell you."

"Something round and pink with a lot of banana in it?" said Deborah. "Can you mean the jelly?"

"Yes," said Teddy Robinson. "Don't look now, but I *think* the teddy-bear brooch is inside that."

"Good gracious!" said Deborah. "How ever did that happen?"

"He fell out of your dress when you were dropping the fruit in it," said Teddy Robinson. "I saw the pin was undone and I didn't tell you, because I wanted you to lose him."

"But why?" asked Deborah.

"Because you'd already got me, and I didn't think you needed another bear," said Teddy Robinson.

"Oh, you silly boy!" said Deborah. "How could you think I'd ever love a silly little teddy bear on a brooch as much as I love you?"

"Think of something round and pink"

Teddy Robinson was very pleased to hear Deborah say this.

"But you mustn't call him silly," he said. "He's mine now, and he's really rather special. I do hope he hasn't melted. Ask Mummy to start serving the jelly, then perhaps we'll find him."

So Mummy began to serve the jelly, and a moment later what should she find but the little teddy-bear brooch, all among the cherries and slices of banana! She was very surprised.

"How ever did he get there?" she said.

"He fell in when I was dropping the fruit in," said Deborah. "Teddy Robinson has just told me so."

"Well, fancy that!" said Auntie Sue. "So he can

have his brooch after all."

Then they washed the teddy-bear brooch, and dried him, and he was pinned on to Teddy Robinson's trouser-strap; and Teddy Robinson said "Thank you" to Auntie Sue for such a nice present. He was very pleased, because the teddy-bear brooch looked as good as new. He hadn't melted a bit, and his silver eyes still sparkled and shone, just as if he'd never been inside a jelly at all.

And that is the end of the story about
Teddy Robinson and the teddy-bear brooch.

7

Teddy Robinson
is Brave

One day Teddy Robinson woke up in the morning feeling very brave and jolly. Even before Deborah was awake he began singing a little song, telling himself all about how brave he was. It went like this:

> *"Jolly brave me,*
> *jolly brave me,*
> *the bravest bear*
> *you ever did see;*
>
> *as brave as a lion*
> *or tiger could be,*
> *as brave as a dragon –*
> *oh, jolly brave me!"*

And by the time Deborah woke up he was

beginning to think he was quite the bravest bear in the whole world.

"Whatever is all this shouting and puffing and blowing?" asked Deborah, opening her eyes sleepily.

"Me fighting a dragon," said Teddy Robinson, puffing out his chest:

> *"Bang, bang, bang, you're dead,*
> *sang the Brave Bear on the bed.*
> *The dragon trembled, sobbed, and sighed,*
> *'Oh, save my life!' he cried . . . and died."*

"Bang, bang, bang, you're dead"

"You see? I killed him!" said Teddy Robinson.

"But I don't see any dragon," said Deborah.

"No, he's gone now," said Teddy Robinson. "Shall we get up? It's quite safe."

Halfway through the morning the phone-bell rang. Mummy was busy, so Deborah lifted the receiver, but before she had time to say "hallo" Teddy Robinson said, "I'll take it! It may be someone ringing up to ask me to fight a dragon." And he said, "Hallo," in a deep, brave growl.

"Hallo," said Daddy's voice, "that's Teddy Robinson, isn't it? How are you?"

"I'm better, thank you," said Teddy Robinson.

"Oh, I didn't know you'd been ill," said Daddy.

"I haven't," said Teddy Robinson.

"Then how can you be better?" said Daddy.

"I'm not better than ill," said Teddy Robinson. "I'm better than better."

"I see," said Daddy. "Now, will you tell Mummy I shall be back early today? And listen, I have a plan—"

"This isn't really me talking," said Teddy Robinson. "It's Deborah. Did you know?"

"I guessed it might be," said Daddy. "But it's you I want to talk to. How would you like to meet me for tea at Black's farm – and bring Deborah too, of course?"

"Will there be a dragon there?" asked Teddy Robinson.

"A what?" said Daddy.

Deborah pushed Teddy Robinson's nose away from the phone and talked to Daddy herself. "Oh, yes!" she said. "It would be lovely. Hold on and I'll fetch Mummy."

When Mummy had finished talking to Daddy and deciding where they should meet she said, "Won't that be nice? It's a long while since we had a walk in the country."

"Will you like it, Teddy Robinson?" asked Deborah.

"I'm just wondering," said Teddy Robinson. "A walk in the country seems rather a soppy way for a Big Brave Bear to spend the afternoon."

"Nonsense," said Deborah. "Daddy is much bigger and braver than you, and he doesn't think so. Shall I ask Andrew to come with us?"

"Not if he brings Spotty," said Teddy Robinson.

"No," said Deborah, "we'll ask him to bring someone else instead."

Andrew said he would like to come, and he would bring his clockwork mouse, who was small and easy to carry.

"A walk in the country will do her good," said

Andrew. "She had rather a fright yesterday with a cat who thought she was real and chased her under the sofa."

So after dinner they all set off.

Deborah and Andrew were excited to be going into the country. Teddy Robinson was still feeling very jolly and big and brave, but Mouse was a little trembly. She had really had quite a fright with the cat the day before.

"Are you sure we shan't run into danger?" she kept asking.

"Don't you worry," said Teddy Robinson. "I'm quite brave enough for two of us and I'll look after you. There's no need to worry while you're with me."

"Thank you," said Mouse. "I'm sure I shall be quite safe with such a big, brave bear as you. I was only thinking – suppose it should thunder?"

"Well, what if it did?" said Teddy Robinson. "*I* shouldn't mind. I love thunder."

"Or what if we should meet some cows?" said Mouse.

"Well, what if we did?" said Teddy Robinson. "*I* aren't frightened of cows. I should just walk bravely past and stare at them fiercely." He began singing:

"Three cheers for me,
for jolly brave me.
Oh, what a jolly brave bear I be!"

Mouse said, "Hip, hip, hooray," three times over in a high, quavering voice. Then she said, "Oh, yes – certainly, and I know now how brave you are. A fly settled on your nose while you were singing, and you never even blinked."

"Pooh! That's nothing," said Teddy Robinson. "I killed a dragon before breakfast."

"Whatever is Teddy Robinson talking about?" said Andrew to Deborah. "What's the matter with him today?"

"I really don't know," said Deborah. "He woke up like it. I'm afraid he's showing off."

When they got out into the open country Mouse and Teddy Robinson were put into Mummy's basket so that Andrew and Deborah could run about freely. They had a lovely time.

But soon a large black cloud came up, and there was a low rumbling noise in the distance.

"Oo-err," said Mouse, "I'm sure that's thunder. Are you frightened of thunder, Teddy Robinson?"

"What, me? I should hope not!" said Teddy Robinson. (There was another low rumble.) "No – I hope not. Yes – I very much hope not."

Deborah and Andrew came running up, saying, "Look at that big black cloud!"

"Yes," said Mummy, "I don't much like the look of it."

"Deborah," said Teddy Robinson, "are you frightened of thunder?"

"Mummy," said Deborah, "are you?"

"No," said Mummy, "but I think we ought to get under cover as soon as possible."

Deborah turned to Teddy Robinson, "Not much," she said, "but we ought to get under cover as soon as possible."

Teddy Robinson turned to Mouse, "No, *I* aren't frightened of thunder," he said, "but I've decided we ought to get under cover as soon as possible."

Then they all began to run.

It wasn't a very bad storm and it hardly rained at all, but Mummy thought they had better hurry.

"We will take a short cut through this field," she said.

"Oo-err," said Mouse, "but there are cows in that field. Do you like cows, Teddy Robinson?"

"Oh, yes," said Teddy Robinson, "I think I like cows. I'll just find out. Deborah, do you like cows?"

"Mummy," said Deborah, "do you like cows?"

"Oh, yes," said Mummy, "of course I do. They are dear, gentle animals, and they give us milk. Don't you like them?"

"Oh, yes," said Deborah, "I like them too. Don't you, Teddy Robinson?"

"Oh, yes," said Teddy Robinson, "I like them very much. At least, I hope I do."

He turned to Mouse. "Of course I like cows," he said. "I'd forgotten for the minute how much I like them. They give us dear, gentle milk. Don't you like them?"

"Yes – I do if you do," said Mouse.

"Oh, I *love* cows," said Teddy Robinson.

"So do I," said Deborah.

"So do I," said Mouse, in a high, trembly voice.

"But I think," said Teddy Robinson, "I think it would be kinder if we all went *round* the field instead of walking though it. We don't want to disturb the poor, dear cows, do we?"

"Oh, no, we don't want to disturb them," said Deborah. "Let's go round by the hedge, then we can look for blackberries. *Please,* Mummy, let's go round by the hedge!"

So they all hurried round the edge of the field (much too quickly to look for blackberries) until they came to the gate on the other side. The cows watched them pass.

"I didn't see you staring at them fiercely," said Mouse to Teddy Robinson, as they went through into the lane.

"How could I? There wasn't time, with everyone running so fast," said Teddy Robinson.

They crossed the lane, and there on the far side of another field they saw Black's farm.

"Come along," said Mummy, "we'll climb over the gate and cut across this field. I expect Daddy will be waiting."

Halfway across the field a cow that they hadn't seen rose from its knees and came walking towards them.

"Oo-err," said Mouse, "run!"

The cow began galloping.

"Oh, dear!" said Teddy Robinson. "Why did you tell it to run?"

"It's all right," said Mummy, "there's nothing to be frightened of."

But Deborah said, "Run, Mummy!" And Andrew said, "Yes, let's run!" And before they had time to think about it they were all running as fast as they could.

Mouse and Teddy Robinson bounced up and down inside the basket until they were quite out of

"I didn't see you staring at them fiercely"

breath, and then all of a sudden a dreadful thing happened. Teddy Robinson bounced so high that he never came down in the basket at all. He came down in the grass, and there were Mummy and Deborah and Andrew still running farther and farther away from him towards the gate on the other side of the field. And the cow was coming nearer and nearer, puffing and galloping and snorting through its nose.

Poor Teddy Robinson! He couldn't do anything

"Eat me now and get it over"

but just lie there and wait for it. He had forgotten all about how to be brave.

"And to think it was only this morning I killed a dragon!" he said to himself. "Or did I? Perhaps it was only a pretend dragon, after all. Yes, now I come to think of it, I'm sure it was only a pretend dragon. But this is a terribly real cow – I can feel its hooves shaking the ground. Oh, my goodness, here it comes!"

The cow came thundering up, then bent its head down and sniffed at Teddy Robinson.

"Please don't wait," said Teddy Robinson. "Eat me now and get it over."

"Mm-m-merr!" said the cow. "Must I?"

"Don't you want to?" said Teddy Robinson. "I thought that was what you were coming for."

"No," said the cow, "I was only coming to see who you were. Mm-m-merr! What a funny little cow you are. I never saw a cow like you before."

"I'm not a little cow," said Teddy Robinson. "I'm a middling-sized teddy bear."

"Why are you looking at me with your eyes crossed?" said the cow.

"I'm not. I'm staring at you fiercely."

"Mm-m-merr," said the cow. "I shouldn't if I were you. The wind might change and they might get stuck."

"Why don't you say Moo?" said Teddy Robinson.

"Because I'm a country cow. Only storybook cows say Moo, not real cows."

"Fancy that!" said Teddy Robinson. "And are you fierce?"

"Terribly fierce," said the cow.

Teddy Robinson trembled all over again.

"Yes," said the cow, "I eat grass and lie in the sun and look at the buttercups. . . ."

"I don't call that very fierce," said Teddy Robinson.

"Well, I'm sorry," said the cow, "but that's all the fierce I know how to be. I told you I'm a country cow. I'm only used to a quiet life."

"Well, thank goodness for that!" said Teddy Robinson. "Now tell me about life in the country."

"Mm-m-merr," said the cow, "it's very quiet, very quiet indeed. Listen to it."

Teddy Robinson listened, and all he could hear was the sound of the grasses rustling in the breeze, and the cow breathing gently through its nose.

"Yes," he said, "it is very quiet, ve-ry qui-et, ve-ry . . ." and a moment later he was asleep.

It seemed hours later that Farmer Black found him in the field, and he was taken into the farmhouse. And there were Deborah and Daddy and Mummy and Andrew and Mouse, all waiting for him, and all terribly glad to see him again.

"Oh, dear Teddy Robinson!" cried Deborah, "I *am* so glad you're not lost. And *what* a brave bear you are! I am sorry I said you were showing off."

"Yes, he really is brave," said Andrew to Daddy. "We all ran away, and only Teddy Robinson was brave enough to face the cow all by himself."

"And stare at him fiercely," squeaked Mouse.

Then Daddy said Teddy Robinson ought to have a medal, and he made one out of a silver milk-bottle top, and Deborah pinned it on to his braces, and everyone said, "Three cheers for Teddy Robinson, our Best Big Brave Brown Bear!"

And that is the end of the story about how
Teddy Robinson was brave.

– 8 –

Teddy Robinson
Has a Holiday

One day in summer it was very, very hot. Teddy Robinson sat on the window-sill in Deborah's room and said to himself, "Phew! Phew! I wish I could take my fur coat off. It *is* a hot day!"

Deborah came running in from the garden to fetch her sun hat. When she saw Teddy Robinson sitting all humpy and hot on the window-sill she said, "Never mind, poor boy. You'll be cooler when you have your holiday."

"Are I going to have a holiday?" said Teddy Robinson.

"Yes, of course you are," said Deborah.

"When will it come?" said Teddy Robinson.

"Very soon now," said Deborah, and she ran out into the garden again.

Teddy Robinson sat and thought about this for a long while. He knew he had heard the word

'holiday' before, but he just could not remember
what it meant.

"Now, I wonder what a holiday can be," he said
to himself. "She said I would be cooler when I had it.
Is it a teddy bear's sun-suit perhaps? Or a little
umbrella? Or could it be a long, cold drink in a glass
with a straw? And she said it would come very soon.
But how will it come? Will it come in a box tied up
with ribbon? Or on a tray? Or will the postman bring
it in a parcel? Or will it just come walking in all by
itself?"

Teddy Robinson didn't know the answer to any of
these questions, so he began singing a little song to
himself.

> *"I'm going to have a holiday,*
> *a holiday,*
> *a holiday.*
> *I'm going to have a holiday.*
> *How lucky I shall be.*
>
> *What ever is a holiday,*
> *a holiday,*
> *a holiday?*
> *What ever is a holiday?*
> *I'll have to wait and see."*

"Yes," he said to himself, "I'll have to wait and see. I'll ask Deborah about it tomorrow."

But when tomorrow came all sorts of exciting things began to happen, so Teddy Robinson forgot to ask Deborah after all.

Daddy brought a big trunk down from the attic, and Mummy began packing it with clothes and shoes, and Deborah turned everything out of her toy-cupboard on to the floor, and began looking for her bucket and spade.

"What's going to happen?" asked Teddy Robinson. "Are we going away?"

"Yes, of course we are," said Deborah. "We're going to the seaside. I told you yesterday."

"How funny. I didn't know," said Teddy Robinson.

"That's why everything is going in the trunk," said Deborah. "To go to the seaside!"

"Us too?" said Teddy Robinson.

"No," said Deborah. "We shall go in a train. Now, be a good boy and help me tidy up all these toys. I've found my bucket and spade."

So together they tidied up the toys. Then they said goodbye to all the dolls and put them to bed in the toy-cupboard.

At last there was nothing left on the floor at all,

except one tiny little round glass thing that Teddy Robinson found lying close beside him. It was about as big as a sixpence, and was a beautiful golden brown colour, with a black blob in the middle.

He showed it to Deborah.

"Now, I wonder what ever that can be," she said. "It can't be a bead, because it hasn't got a hole through the middle."

"Now I wonder what ever that can be"

"And it can't be a marble," said Teddy Robinson, "because it's flat on one side."

"Perhaps it's a sweet," said Deborah.

"Suck it and see," said Teddy Robinson.

"I mustn't suck it in case it's poison," said Deborah. So she licked it instead.

"No," she said, "it isn't a sweet, because it hasn't got any taste."

"It's very pretty," said Teddy Robinson. "Shall we keep it?"

"Yes," said Deborah. "It's too pretty to throw away. I wish I could think what it is, though. I'm sure I've seen it before somewhere, but I can't remember where."

"That's funny," said Teddy Robinson. "I was thinking just the same thing."

Before they went to bed that night they dropped the pretty little round thing (that wasn't a marble, and wasn't a bead, and wasn't a sweet) through the slot in Deborah's money-box.

"That will be a safe place to keep it," said Deborah.

And the very next day they all went away to the seaside.

Teddy Robinson enjoyed the ride in the train very much, because he was allowed to sit in the rack and look after the luggage. And Deborah enjoyed it very much, because they had a picnic dinner in the train, and it was so lovely to be able to look out of the window and watch the cows in the fields and eat a hard-boiled egg in her fingers at the same time.

It wasn't until they were quite half-way there

that things began to go wrong.

Daddy lifted Teddy Robinson down from the rack. He was just going to give him to Deborah when he looked at him closely and said, "Hallo, old man, what's happened to your other eye?"

"Oh dear," said Mummy. "Is it loose? I shall have to sew it on again before it gets lost."

"No, it isn't here," said Daddy.

"Oh dear! Oh dear!" said Deborah. "Let me see. Oh, you poor boy! What are we to do? Wherever can it be?"

They all began looking round the railway carriage and in the corners of the seats, but the other eye was nowhere to be seen.

Deborah lifted Teddy Robinson on to her lap to comfort him and looked sadly into his one eye. Suddenly she said, "Teddy Robinson! Do you remember the pretty little round glass thing we found yesterday?"

"The thing that wasn't a bead, and wasn't a marble, and wasn't a sweet?" said Teddy Robinson.

"Yes," said Deborah. "Well, that was your eye! This one is just the same. Fancy my not knowing it when I saw it!"

"And it's in the money-box," said Teddy Robinson sadly.

"Oh dear, so it is!" said Deborah. "What ever shall we do?"

"Stop the train!" said Teddy Robinson. "We must go home and fetch it at once."

But they couldn't stop the train. Daddy and Mummy both said they couldn't. So Teddy Robinson sat in the corner seat and grumbled to himself quietly while Deborah tried to comfort him by telling him about the nice time he was going to have at the seaside.

"We'll go down to the beach every day," she said, "and you shall come with me. Don't mind about

"Stop the train!"

your eye too much. You shall have it as soon as we get home."

"But I can't go down to the beach with only one eye," said Teddy Robinson.

"Yes, you can," said Deborah. "No one will notice."

"No, I can't," said Teddy Robinson. "There will be other children on the beach. If I can't go with two eyes I won't go at all."

"Oh, Teddy Robinson," said Deborah. "What am I to do with you?"

"I know!" said Daddy. "Make him into a pirate. Pirates always wear a patch over one eye. Then no one will know."

"Yes," said Mummy. "What a good idea! And he can wear my red-and-white spotted handkerchief round his head."

"And he can wear curtain rings for ear-rings," said Deborah. "Yes, that *is* a good idea."

Teddy Robinson began to feel much happier, and by the time the train came into the station his one eye was twinkling as usual, and he felt as pleased as Deborah to think they were really at the seaside at last.

As soon as breakfast was over the next morning Teddy Robinson and Deborah got ready to go down to the beach.

Deborah wore shorts and a T-shirt, and Teddy Robinson wore his trousers and no shirt. Mummy fixed the patch over his eye, and hung two gold curtain rings over his ears with pieces of cotton. Then she tied her red-and-white spotted handkerchief round his head.

"There, now," she said; "doesn't he look exactly like a pirate?" And she called Daddy to come and see.

"My word!" said Daddy. "I hope he won't frighten everybody away!"

On the way down to the beach Teddy Robinson said to Deborah, "Do I really look like a pirate?"

"Yes," said Deborah, "you really do."

"What *is* a pirate?" asked Teddy Robinson.

"He's a fierce robber man who lives in a ship," said Deborah.

"Oh, goody! I love being fierce," said Teddy Robinson. "And who do I rob?"

"Other people who live in other ships," said Deborah.

"That will be very nice," said Teddy Robinson. "I hope there will be plenty of other people in other ships there."

But when they got down to the beach they found that the other people were mostly sitting about in deckchairs or walking about on the sands.

"I can't very well rob people who're sitting in deckchairs, can I?" said Teddy Robinson. "And I don't think I should look quite right sitting in one myself."

So Daddy and Deborah made a big sandcastle down by the edge of the sea, and when it was finished they sat Teddy Robinson on top of it.

"There," said Deborah. "Your ship has been wrecked and sunk to the bottom of the sea, but you are safe on a desert island all of your own. Now you don't mind if I go and play with the other children, do you?"

Teddy Robinson didn't mind a bit. When Deborah had gone he sat on top of his sandcastle island and looked out to sea, feeling very fierce and brave.

He watched the seagulls flying and diving over the waves. After a while one of them came flying round and swooped down quite close to his head, screaming at him. It sounded very fierce, but Teddy Robinson didn't mind because he was feeling fierce too.

"Who are you-ou-ou?" screamed the seagull. "And what are you doing here?"

"I'm a pirate," shouted Teddy Robinson, "and I'm not afraid of you, even if you do scream at me. This is my very own island, and you can't come on it."

"I'm not afraid of you even if you do scream at me"

The seagull screamed at him again and flew away.

Then a crab came waddling round the sandcastle island. It walked sideways and looked up at Teddy Robinson with cross black eyes.

"Who are you?" said the crab. "And what are you doing on my beach?"

"I'm a pirate," roared Teddy Robinson in a big, brave bear's voice, "and I'm not afraid of you, even if you do walk sideways and stare at me with a cross face. And this is *my* island, so you can't come on it unless I invite you."

"Are you going to invite me?" said the crab.

"Not unless you stop looking so cross," said Teddy Robinson.

"Then I shan't come," said the crab. "If I want to be cross I *shall* be cross, and even a pirate can't stop me."

And he scuttled away into the sand.

Teddy Robinson felt very happy indeed. There was nothing he liked better than spending a beautiful, fierce morning all by himself at the seaside.

He began singing about it as loudly as he could.

> *"Look at me*
> *beside the sea,*
> *the one-eyed pirate bear!*

It looked up at him with cross black eyes

You'll never be
as fierce as me,
so fight me if you dare!"

Just then a big black dog came running down the beach and began barking loudly at Teddy Robinson.

"Woof! Woof! What are you doing?" he barked.

"I'm a pirate on a desert island," shouted Teddy Robinson, "and you can't frighten me, even if you do bark at me so rudely."

"Woof! Woof!" barked the dog. "You certainly are on an island. Look, there's water all round you."

"Good gracious, so there is!" said Teddy Robinson. "However did that happen?"

"I expect the tide came up when you weren't looking," said the big black dog. "Woof! Woof! Shall I save you?"

"No, thank you," said Teddy Robinson. "Pirates don't need to be saved. But thank you for telling me."

He was just beginning to wonder how he was going to get back to the beach all by himself when Deborah came running up and paddled out to the castle to fetch him.

"Oh, Teddy Robinson!" she said. "I heard the dog barking, and I got quite a fright when I saw you sitting

"You certainly are on an island!"

with the water all round you. Were you frightened when you saw the tide was coming up?"

"Of course I weren't," said Teddy Robinson. "Pirates aren't frightened. I was just looking out to sea with my one brave eye and I never even noticed it. You know, I'm very fond of my other eye, but I'm rather glad we left it at home after all. I do so like being a pirate at the seaside. Can I have a castle to myself every day?"

"Yes, every day till we go home," said Deborah. "But next time we won't put it so near the edge of the water."

When at last the holiday was over and they all went home again Teddy Robinson was quite excited to find his other eye still inside Deborah's money-box, and to have it sewn on again. He and Deborah both felt as if they had been away for years and years, because everyone at home seemed so pleased to see them again.

"How big you've grown!" they all said to Deborah, and "How brown you are!" they all said to Teddy Robinson. "What a lovely holiday you must have had."

"Oh! My holiday!" said Teddy Robinson. "I'd forgotten all about it!"

"What do you mean?" said Deborah.

"Well, I never had it, did I?" said Teddy Robinson. "Did it come while we were at the seaside?"

"Of course it did," said Deborah. "That *was* your holiday – going to the seaside."

"Well, I never!" said Teddy Robinson. "Was it really? Oh, I *am* glad if *that* was my holiday. I never thought it would be anything as nice as that!"

And that is the end of the story about how
Teddy Robinson had a holiday.

9

Teddy Robinson Goes to Hospital

Once upon a time Teddy Robinson and Deborah went to hospital. They didn't know a bit what it was going to be like because neither of them had ever been before, so they were glad to have each other for company.

A kind nurse in a white cap and apron tucked them up in a little white bed in a big room called the ward, and while Mummy was in another room talking to the doctor they lay side by side and whispered to each other, and looked around to see what hospital was like.

There were a lot of other children in the ward as well. Some of them were in little white beds like Deborah and Teddy Robinson, and some of them were dressed and running around in soft bedroom slippers.

There were coloured pictures of nursery rhyme

people all round the walls, and quite close to Deborah's bed there was a big glass tank full of water with a lot of tiny fish swimming around inside. It was called an aquarium.

Teddy Robinson liked this, and so did Deborah. After a while they sat up so that they could see better, and they watched the fish swimming round and round until Mummy came in to say goodbye.

They were rather sad to say goodbye, but Mummy promised she would come and see them again next day, and when she had gone Deborah comforted Teddy Robinson, and Teddy Robinson comforted Deborah, and a nice kind nurse came and comforted them both, so they didn't need to be sad after all.

A little boy in the next bed said, "What's your name? I'm called Tommy. Would your bear like to talk to my horse?" And he pulled out a little brown felt horse from under the blanket and threw it over to Deborah's bed.

"His name's Cloppety," he said.

"Thank you," said Deborah. "My name is Deborah, and this is Teddy Robinson," and she sat them side by side with their noses close together so they could make friends with each other.

Teddy Robinson and Cloppety stared hard at

each other for quite a long while, then they began to talk quietly.

"Been here long?" asked Teddy Robinson.

"Been here long?"

"About a week," said Cloppety. "We're going home soon because Tommy's nearly better; he's getting up tomorrow. Why are you only wearing a vest?"

"I don't know," said Teddy Robinson. "Deborah forgot my trousers."

"What a pity," said Cloppety. "I had to leave my cart at home, so I know what it feels like. Are you happy here?"

"Yes," said Teddy Robinson, "I like watching the fish."

"So do I," said Cloppety.

When evening came and all the children were tucked up for the night it was very cosy in the ward. Little lights were left burning so that it was never quite dark, and Teddy Robinson and Deborah lay and watched the nurses going round to all the beds and cots and tucking up each of the children in turn. Cloppety had gone back to Tommy's bed, so they snuggled down together just as they did at home.

"Dear old boy," said Deborah. "I'm glad you're with me. Isn't Tommy a nice boy?"

"Yes," said Teddy Robinson, "and Cloppety's a nice horse."

And quite soon they were both fast asleep.

The next day Tommy was up, and running around in bedroom slippers like the other children who were nearly better, so for quite a lot of the day Cloppety stayed with Teddy Robinson, and Tommy came to see Deborah every now and then, and brought her toys and books from the hospital toy-cupboard.

Mummy came to see them, and she brought a red shoulder-bag with a zip-fastener for Deborah, and a real little nightshirt (made out of Deborah's old pyjamas) for Teddy Robinson. She also brought his old trousers that had got left behind by mistake.

They were very pleased. Deborah wore the shoulder-bag sitting up in bed, and Teddy Robinson put on his new nightie straight away.

"That's nice," said Cloppety, peeping over the bedclothes when Mummy had gone.

"Yes," said Teddy Robinson. "It's just what I was needing. Do you wish you had one?"

"Horses don't bother with nighties," said Cloppety. "I wish you could have seen my cart, though. It's green with yellow wheels, and the wheels really go round."

But Teddy Robinson wasn't listening. He was beginning to make up a little song in his head, all about his new nightie. And this is how it went:

> *"Highty tiddly ighty,*
> *a teddy bear wearing a nightie*
> *can feel he's dressed*
> *and looking his best*
> *(he couldn't do that in only a vest),*
> *highty tiddly ighty."*

In a few days the doctor said Deborah was better, and she was allowed to get up and run about the ward with the other children who were dressed; but Teddy Robinson still liked his nightie so much better than his vest and trousers that he decided he wasn't well enough to get up yet.

"Shall I dress you, too, Teddy Robinson?" asked Deborah.

"No, thank you," he said. "I think I'll stay in my nightie and sit on the pillow. I can watch you from there, and it will rest my legs."

The next day Tommy went home because he was quite well again, and Teddy Robinson and Deborah were quite sorry when he and Cloppety came to say goodbye. All the rest of that day his bed looked so empty that they didn't like looking at it.

"Never mind, Teddy Robinson," said Deborah. "We'll be going home ourselves soon." And they went off together to play with the other children.

Those who were up and nearly better had their meals at a little table at the other end of the ward, so it wasn't until after tea that Teddy Robinson and Deborah came back to their own bed. When they did they were surprised to see a new little girl lying in Tommy's bed.

"Hallo," said Deborah. "You weren't here before tea."

"No," said the little girl. "I've only just come, and I want to go home," and she looked as if she might be going to cry.

So Deborah said, "I expect you *will* go home soon. But it's nice here." And then she told her all about the hospital, and showed her the aquarium, and the little girl told her that her name was Betty, and soon they were quite like best friends.

"I wish I'd brought my doll," said Betty, looking at Teddy Robinson. "I came in a hurry and forgot her. Mummy's going to bring her tomorrow, but I want her now," and she looked as if she might cry again.

"You'd better have my teddy for a little while," said Deborah. "He's nice to cuddle if you're feeling sad. But don't cry all over his fur. He doesn't like it."

So Teddy Robinson got into bed beside Betty. He didn't talk to her because he was shy and didn't know her, but Betty seemed to like him and soon her eyes closed and she fell asleep hugging him.

When it was Deborah's bedtime she didn't like to take Teddy Robinson back in case she woke Betty, so she asked the nurse who came to tuck her up. The nurse went over to Betty's bed and looked at her and then she came back to Deborah.

"Would you mind very much if she kept him just for tonight?" she said. "She is fast asleep, and it seems such a pity to wake her. It would be awfully kind if you could lend him."

So Deborah said she would, and Teddy Robinson stayed where he was.

Deborah soon dropped off to sleep, but Teddy Robinson didn't. He lay in Betty's bed and watched the night-nurse who was writing at a little table, and looked at the fish swimming round and round in the aquarium, and then he began to sing to himself very softly, and after a while when he was sure that all the children were asleep he rolled over, tumbled gently out of bed, and rolled a little way across the floor.

At that moment a baby in a cot woke up and began to cry. The night-nurse stopped writing and came quickly down the ward to see who it was. As she passed Teddy Robinson her foot bumped against him and she nearly fell over him. She bent down and picked him up and then hurried on to comfort the crying baby.

As soon as the baby saw Teddy Robinson he stopped crying and said, "Teddy, teddy," so the nurse put Teddy Robinson inside the cot and let the baby hold him. But when she tried to take him back the baby started crying again, so after a while the nurse left him there, hoping he would help the baby go to sleep, and she went back to her writing.

But the baby didn't go to sleep. Instead he began pulling Teddy Robinson's arms and legs and ears, and poking his fingers in his eyes. Teddy Robinson didn't mind much because it didn't hurt him, but after a while the baby pulled his right ear so that it nearly came off, and instead of sticking up on top of his head like the other ear it hung down with only a thread of cotton holding it on.

"I bet I look silly," he said to himself. "I wonder what Deborah will say." And he felt rather sorry about it.

In the morning when the children all woke up Deborah and Betty didn't know wherever Teddy Robinson could be. They looked everywhere in both their beds, but of course they couldn't find him. So as soon as she was dressed Deborah began going round the ward looking at all the children's beds and peeping into all the babies' cots. And when she came to the cot where he was she could hardly believe it!

The baby was fast asleep at last, but there was poor Teddy Robinson peeping through the bars with one ear hanging right down over his eye.

"You poor old boy," she said. "What *are* you doing in there? You look as if you're in a cage. Wait a minute and I'll get you out."

She had to ask a nurse to lift him out of the cot, and then she hugged him and kissed him and carried him back to her own bed.

—peeping through the bars with one ear hanging right down—

"Oh, Teddy Robinson," she said, "how did you get there? And what *has* happened to your poor ear? It's only hanging on by one little piece of cotton."

"I think you'd better pull it off," said Teddy Robinson bravely, "otherwise I might lose it."

"All right," said Deborah, "and I'll keep it for you till we get home; then we'll ask Mummy to mend it."

Then she gave the ear a sharp little tug and off it came.

"You're a dear brave boy," said Deborah, and she kissed the place where it had been, and put the ear carefully away in her shoulder-bag.

When the night-nurse came round that evening and saw Teddy Robinson sitting on the pillow with only one ear she remembered what had happened the night before, and she told Deborah all about it; how she had nearly fallen over him and had given him to the baby to stop him crying.

"But I *am* sorry about his ear," she said.

"It's all right," said Deborah. "I've got it safely in my shoulder-bag, and we're going home tomorrow, so Mummy will mend it."

"I'm so glad," said the nurse. "I was wondering if he would like it bandaged."

Deborah knew that Teddy Robinson would simply love that, so she said, "Oh, yes, please!" And the nurse bandaged Teddy Robinson's head round and round with a piece of real hospital bandage. He didn't mind a bit that one eye got covered up at the same time, and when it was finished both Deborah and the nurse said he looked lovely.

Early next morning Teddy Robinson was dressed in his vest and trousers again, and his nightie was packed away with his ear in Deborah's shoulder-bag. Mummy came to fetch them, and they said goodbye to everybody, even the fish in the aquarium.

She bandaged his head

131

They were both very pleased to be going home again, and Teddy Robinson was specially pleased because he was going out with a real bandage on. He couldn't help hoping that everyone would notice it, because then they would all know that he had been in a real hospital!

And that is the end of the story about how
Teddy Robinson went to hospital.

10

Teddy Robinson's
Concert Party

One day Teddy Robinson was lying on his back in front of the fire with Deborah's cousin Philip. Suddenly Philip tickled him in the tummy and said, "I say, Teddy R! Let's make a surprise. I feel like doing something funny."

"Oh, so do I!" said Teddy Robinson. "Where's Deborah?"

"She's gone to ask Andrew and Mary-Anne to tea today," said Philip. "Let's think of something to do when they come."

"I suppose I couldn't have another birthday party?" said Teddy Robinson.

"No," said Philip. "We must think of something new. Couldn't we do some tricks?"

"I know!" said Teddy Robinson. "Ask them to sit down to listen to a story, and then when they're all waiting you just fly out of the window. That would be a jolly good trick!"

"But I can't fly." said Philip.

"Oh, no. Bother! We can't do that then."

"Think of something else," said Philip.

"Make faces at them," said Teddy Robinson.

"That wouldn't be funny enough to make them laugh."

"The face you're making now would make anyone laugh," said Teddy Robinson.

"I'm not making a face. This is my ordinary one."

"Well, it's different from usual," said Teddy Robinson.

"That's because I'm thinking. Don't be silly."

"Well, then," said Teddy Robinson, "don't let's try to be funny. Let's do something Sweet and Beautiful and a little bit Sad, like the Babes in the Wood."

"No," said Philip. "Let's have something jolly, even if we can't be funny. Think again."

"*I* know!" said Teddy Robinson. "I'll have a concert party!"

Philip thought this was a fine idea. When Deborah came back he and Teddy Robinson told her all about it.

"I'm going to sing songs," said Teddy Robinson, "and say pieces of poetry, and we'll have some refreshments, and then I'll do conjuring tricks."

"But what's Philip going to do?" asked Deborah.

"Help *me*," said Teddy Robinson. "It's *my* concert party."

"And are you going to make the refreshments too?"

"No," he said, "you know I can't do that; but you're going to be very kind, like you always are, and ask Mummy."

Mummy said, yes, she would make the refreshments. They could have raisins (six each) and chocolate biscuits (cut in halves) and dolly mixture (handed round in a bowl).

Philip began making the programme, and Teddy Robinson sat beside him and told him what to write. Deborah brought the dolls out of the toy-cupboard and tidied them up.

"You can be the audience." she said.

The stage was a great trouble, until Mummy had a good idea.

Why not turn the kitchen table on its side?" she said. "You can have it in here, just for the afternoon." She gave them some old curtains and a bunch of chrysanthemums.

"The flowers aren't very fresh," she said, "but you might use them for decoration. And you can hang the curtains on a string and tie the ends to the table-legs."

Teddy Robinson told him what to write —

While Philip and Deborah got the stage ready Teddy Robinson sat thinking hard about all the things he was going to do.

"Are you sure you don't want anyone else to do anything?" asked Deborah. "It's rather a lot for one."

"No, thank you," said Teddy Robinson; "but I might have Jacqueline in one scene. Is Mary-Anne bringing her?"

(Jacqueline was Mary-Anne's beautiful doll.)

"Yes," said Deborah, "and Andrew is bringing his toy dog, Spotty. You might use him too?"

"No," said Teddy Robinson. "He argues too much."

When Mary-Anne and Andrew arrived, with Jacqueline and the spotted dog, they found the stage all set up ready. The curtains were hung on a string across the front, and the bunch of flowers hung from the middle, just where the curtains met. (You will see in the picture how it looked.)

In front of the stage all the dolls were sitting in tidy rows, staring at the curtains, and waiting for the show to begin. A large notice was pinned to the door. It said:

TEDDY ROBINSON'S CONCERT PARTY
Programme

RECITATION, by Teddy Robinson

A SEEN FROM SLEEPING BEAUTY, by Teddy Robinson
and Jacqueline (thought of by Teddy Robinson)

SONG, by Teddy Robinson

REFRESHMENTS, thought of by Teddy Robinson,
handed round by Deborah, made by Mummy

CONJURING TRICKS, by the FAMOUS WIZARD
T. NOSNIBOR (helped by Philip)
Audience arranged by Deborah
No smoking or shouting

Jacqueline was very surprised when Mary-Anne

told her that she was going to be on the stage. She hadn't been able to read the programme herself, because her eyes were shut.

"I'm afraid they're stuck again," whispered Mary-Anne to Deborah. "Will it matter?"

"Not a bit," said Deborah. "She's going to be the Sleeping Beauty."

Jacqueline was hustled behind the stage to where Philip and Teddy Robinson were waiting.

"You're on next," Teddy Robinson told her. "I'm first."

"We're ready to begin now," said Philip.

"About time, too," said the spotted dog, who was rather cross at not being asked to go on the stage as well.

"Hush!" said all the dolls. "They're going to begin."

Teddy Robinson came to the front of the curtain. He bowed low to the audience, then he said:

"Welcome.
  "Ladies and gentlemen,
    what a sight
    to see you sitting here tonight!
    I'm pleased to see you
    every one,
    so clap your hardest when I've done—"

He bowed low to the audience.

This wasn't really the end of the poem, but as everyone started clapping their hardest straight away Teddy Robinson leaned back against the curtain and waited for them to finish. But he had forgotten there was nothing behind the curtain, so a moment later he fell through and disappeared out of sight.

The audience didn't know this was a mistake. Everyone clapped harder than ever, so nobody heard Teddy Robinson saying, in a rather cross voice, "But I haven't finished yet! There's another verse."

"Never mind," said Philip. "Let's do the next scene."

Teddy Robinson's head came out from between the curtains.

"The next scene is Sleeping Beauty," he said, "and please don't clap *till the end*."

After a little waiting Deborah pulled the curtains aside. This was the first time the audence had seen the whole stage, and everyone said, "Oo-oh, isn't it pretty!"

On a pink cushion lay Jacqueline, fast asleep and looking very beautiful. There were two or three ferns in pots, arranged to look like trees, and some leaves from the garden were sprinkled about on the ground. On the other side stood the wooden horse, and on

A scene from Sleeping Beauty

his back, looking very proud and princely, sat Teddy Robinson. He was wearing the dolls' Red-Riding-Hood cloak (with the hood tucked inside), and a beret with a long curly feather (from one of Mummy's old hats) on his head. He also had a sword (cut out of cardboard) and socks rolled down to look like boots.

"How handsome he is!" said all the dolls.

"Huh!" said the spotted dog. "I think he looks soppy."

The horse began to move slowly across the stage towards Jacqueline. Philip was pulling it on a string from the other side; but the string hardly showed at

(thought of by Teddy Robinson)

all, so it looked very real. The dolls all wanted to clap, but they remembered just in time and didn't. The horse, with Teddy Robinson on its back, moved slowly forward until its front wheels came up against the edge of the pink cushion. Then it gave a jerk, and Teddy Robinson fell headlong over its neck and landed beside Jacqueline, with his nose buried in the cushion.

Everyone waited to see what was going to happen next, but nothing happened. They went on waiting. At last Teddy Robinson said, in a muffled, squeaky voice, "It's the end. For goodness sake, clap! I'm suffocating."

Deborah pulled the curtains quickly, and the audience clapped hard.

After a good deal of whispering behind the stage Teddy Robinson's head came out again from between the curtains.

"Ladies and gentlemen," he said, "as you never seem to know when it's the end of anything I'll tell you when to clap next time. The next scene is The Bear in the Wood."

His head disappeared, but shot out again a moment later.

"You can clap now while you're waiting," he said.

When the curtains parted once more Jacqueline

and the cushion had gone, but the leaves and ferns were still there. Teddy Robinson sat under the largest fern. He began singing:

"I'm a poor teddy bear,
growing thinner and thinner.
I haven't any Deborah
to give me any dinner."

The audience loved this. They laughed loudly, because Teddy Robinson looked so very fat and cosy that they thought he was trying to be funny. But Teddy Robinson had meant it to be a sad song. He went on:

"I'm lost in a wood
where the trees are thick and high.
If someone doesn't find me
I might lie down and die."

"Oh dear!" said one of the dolls. "Let me find him! I think he means it."

Teddy Robinson turned to the audience and said:

"I hope you won't get worried
at this sad, sad song.
I'm lying down to die now,
but I shan't stay dead for long."

143

He then lay down in the middle of the stage, and Philip emptied a basketful of leaves over him. Teddy Robinson sang the last verse,

> *"With only leaves to cover me*
> *and grass beneath my head,*
> *that is the end of the Bear in the Wood,*
> *and now I'm really dead. You can clap now."*

The audience clapped and cheered. Some of them thought it was sad, and some of them thought it was funny, but they all loved it. After that it was time for the refreshments.

Philip and Teddy Robinson, behind the curtains, were busy clearing away the leaves and ferns.

"How is it going?" whispered Teddy Robinson.

Philip peeped through the curtain.

"I think it's going jolly well," he said. "They seem to be enjoying the refreshments like anything."

When all was ready, and the last raisin had been eaten, Deborah drew the curtains for the Famous Wizard Nosnibor.

Teddy Robinson was sitting in the middle of the stage. He had a tall white paper hat on his head, and another hat (one of Daddy's) lay on a little table beside him.

"Why is he wearing a dunce's hat?" asked the spotted dog in a loud voice.

"He isn't," whispered Deborah. "It's a wizard's hat."

"Hush!" said all the dolls. "He's going to begin."

Philip handed him a stick covered with silver paper.

"This is my magic wand," said Teddy Robinson in a deep voice, "and I am the famous Wizard Nosnibor."

Then he waved the wand over the hat on the table, and said:

> "Abracadabra,
> titfer-tat.
> You'll find a rabbit
> inside the hat!"

Philip lifted up the hat, and there, underneath it, sat Deborah's stuffed rabbit. All the dolls clapped and said:

"What a wonderful trick!"

But the spotted dog said, "I know how he did that one. He put the rabbit there before we started."

"Hush!" said the dolls. "He's going to do another trick!"

Philip put two little bowls on the ground in front of Teddy Robinson. One was red and the other was white. He turned them both upside down, then he put a marble under the red bowl.

"Which bowl is the marble under?" said Teddy Robinson.

"The red one," everybody shouted.

Teddy Robinson waved his magic wand over the two bowls and said:

> *"Roll, little marble,*
> *roll, roll, roll.*
> *Choose for yourself*
> *your favourite bowl."*

"Oh, *I* know that trick!" shouted the spotted dog. "I saw a man do it at a party. The marble's gone under the other bowl, the white one. *That's* not a new trick!"

Teddy Robinson waited, looking mysterious and important. Philip lifted up the white bowl. There was nothing there. Then he lifted up the red bowl. There was the marble!

"You see," said Teddy Robinson, "it *is* a new trick."

The dolls clapped even harder and cried, "Oh, *isn't* he clever!"

But the spotted dog kept saying, over and over again, "It *wasn't* a new trick. Look here, listen to me—"

The Famous Wizard Nosnibor N

"Andrew," said Deborah, "if you can't keep Spotty quiet I think you'd better take him away."

"Oh, all right," said Andrew. "I'll keep him quiet."

"Now," said Teddy Robinson, "if you've all finished clapping I'll show you my next trick."

"*I* wasn't clapping," said the spotted dog.

"This trick," said Teddy Robinson, "is called The Magic Flowers."

Philip laid a small bunch of flowers on the left-hand side of the stage. Teddy Robinson waved his magic wand and said,

"Snip-snap-snorum, fiddle-de-dee,
hokum-pokum, one-two-three.
Magic Flowers on the floor,
come to Wizard Nosnibor!"

The bunch of flowers began moving slowly across the floor all by itself. The audience clapped and cheered.

Teddy Robinson waved his magic wand once more, and then the biggest and best surprise of all happened. The bunch of chrysanthemums hanging above his head suddenly fell straight down into his lap, and at the same minute the curtains fell down on top of him, covering everything except his nose and one eye. The audience cheered louder than ever.

Teddy Robinson said, "THE END," very slowly and loudly, and bowed beneath the curtains.

There was a great deal of noise after this. The audience was still clapping and cheering, and Philip was shouting, "Hooray for the Famous Wizard!" And Mary-Anne was telling everybody it was the nicest concert party she had ever seen. Only Spotty was still arguing.

"I don't believe there *is* such a person as the Wizard Nosnibor," he said.

"If some people could read other people's names

backwards," said Teddy Robinson, "they wouldn't think they were quite so clever."

Much later on, when it was all over, Deborah said, "Teddy Robinson, that *was* a lovely concert party!"

"Yes, wasn't it?" said Teddy Robinson.

"Do tell me how you did the Magic Flowers," said Deborah.

"A piece of black cotton was tied on them," said Teddy Robinson. "Philip pulled it."

"But how did you get the other flowers and the curtains to fall down at exactly the right minute?"

"I'll tell you a secret," said Teddy Robinson. "I didn't. I think the string broke. You couldn't have been more surprised than I was. Don't tell anyone, will you?"

And that is the end of the story about
Teddy Robinson's concert party.

11

Teddy Robinson and the Beautiful Present

One day Teddy Robinson and Deborah went to Granny's house for the afternoon.

After tea Granny gave Deborah a little round tin, full of soapy stuff, and a piece of bent wire, round at one end and straight at the other end.

"What is it for?" asked Deborah.

"It's for blowing bubbles," said Granny. "I'll show you how to do it." And she dipped the end of the wire into the tin, and then blew gently through it into the air. A whole stream of bubbles flew out into the room.

"Oh!" exclaimed Deborah. "What a Beautiful Present!"

"It will keep you happy till Daddy comes to fetch you," said Granny, and she went away to tidy up the tea things.

Teddy Robinson sat in Granny's armchair and

watched Deborah blowing the bubbles. They were very pretty.

"Can I have one?" he asked.

Deborah blew a bubble at him, and it landed on his arm.

"Oh, thank you," he said. "Can I keep it?"

But before Deborah could say yes, the bubble had made a tiny little splutter and burst.

"Well, I'm blowed!" said Teddy Robinson. "That one's gone. Blow me another!"

So Deborah blew another. This one landed on his foot. But again it spluttered and burst.

"More!" said Teddy Robinson. So Deborah blew a whole stream of bubbles, and they landed all over

— they landed all over him —

him: one on his ear, one on his toe, five or six on his arms and legs, and one on the very end of his nose. But, one by one, they all spluttered and burst. Teddy Robinson's fur was damp where the bubbles had been, and he felt rather cross.

"The ones you give me aren't any good," he said. "They all burst."

"They are meant to burst," said Deborah.

"Then what's the good of them?" said Teddy Robinson.

"Just to look beautiful, for a minute," said Deborah.

"I think that's silly," said Teddy Robinson. "If I couldn't look beautiful for more than a minute without bursting, I wouldn't bother to look beautiful at all. Stop blowing bubbles and play with me instead."

"No, said Deborah. "I can play with you any time. I want to play with my beautiful bubbles just now. Don't bother me, there's a good boy."

So Teddy Robinson sat and sang to himself while he watched Deborah blowing bubbles.

"The trouble
with a bubble
is the way it isn't there
the minute that you've blown it

and thrown it
in the air.
It's a pity,
when you're pretty,
to disappear in air.
I'm glad I'm not a bubble;
I'd rather be a bear."

When it was time to go home Daddy came to fetch them on his bicycle. Deborah ran to show him the Beautiful Present.

"Show me how it works when we get home," said Daddy. "We must hurry now, because Mummy is waiting for us."

So Teddy Robinson and Deborah said goodbye to Granny, and Daddy took them out to the gate where his bicycle was waiting. He popped Teddy Robinson into the basket on the front, then he lifted Deborah up into the little seat at the back, just behind him.

"You carry my Beautiful Present, Daddy," said Deborah. So Daddy put it in his pocket. Then off they all went.

Teddy Robinson loved riding in the bicycle basket. The wind whistled in his fur, and he sang to himself all the way home:

"Head over heels,
how nice it feels,
a basket-y ride
on bicycle wheels."

It was beginning to get dark, and the lights were going on in all the houses when at last they reached home.

"Now run in quickly," said Daddy, as he lifted Deborah down from her little seat. "Here are your bubbles," he said, and he took Granny's present out of his pocket.

Deborah ran in at the front door where Mummy was waiting. Teddy Robinson heard her calling as she ran, "Look, Mummy – I've got such a Beautiful Present!" Then the front door shut behind them.

Daddy wheeled the bicycle round the side of the house to the tool-shed. He opened the door and pushed the bicycle inside, leaning it up against the wall. Then he went out again and shut the door behind him.

"Oh, dear!" said Teddy Robinson. "They've forgotten I'm still in the basket. I expect they'll come back and fetch me later."

But they didn't come back and fetch him, because Daddy had quite forgotten that he had put Teddy

Robinson in the basket, and Deborah thought she must have left him at Granny's house. So she went to bed thinking that Granny would be bringing him back tomorrow.

It was very dark in the tool-shed, and very quiet.

Teddy Robinson smoothed his fur and pulled up his braces, and sang a little song to keep himself company:

> *"Oh, my fur and braces!*
> *How dark it is at night*
> *sitting in the tool-shed*
> *without electric light!*
>
> *Sitting in the tool-shed,*
> *with no one here but me.*
> *Oh, my fur and braces,*
> *what a funny place to be!"*

He rather liked the bit about the fur and braces, so he sang it again. Then he stopped singing and listened to the quietness instead. And after a while he found that it wasn't really quiet at all in the tool-shed. All sorts of little noises and rustlings were going on, very tiny little noises that he wouldn't have noticed if everything else hadn't been so quiet.

—it hung just in front of his nose

First he heard the bustling of a lot of little earwigs running to and fro under a pile of logs in the corner. Then he heard the panting of a crowd of tiny ants who were struggling across the floor with a long twig they were carrying. Then he heard the sigh of a little moth as it shook its wings and fluttered about the windowpane. Teddy Robinson was glad to think he wasn't all by himself in the tool-shed after all.

Suddenly something came dropping down from the ceiling on a long, thin thread and hung just in front of his nose. It made one or two funny faces at him, then pulled itself up again and disappeared out of sight. Teddy Robinson was so frightened that he nearly fell out of the bicycle basket. But then he realized that it was only a spider.

What a pity, he thought. I'd have said Good Evening if I'd known it was coming.

A moment later he felt a gentle plop on top of his head and knew that the spider had come down again. This time he wasn't frightened, only surprised.

It seemed rather silly to say Good Evening to someone who was sitting on top of his head, so Teddy Robinson began singing again, in his smallest voice, just to let the spider know he was there.

"Oh, my fur and braces!
You did give me a fright,
making funny faces
in the middle of the night!

Hanging from the ceiling
by a tiny silver thread,
what a funny feeling
when you landed on my head!"

The spider crawled across the front of Teddy Robinson's head and looked down into one of his eyes.

"I say," he said. "I do beg your pardon. I didn't know it was your head I'd landed on. And when I came down the first time I'd no idea I was making faces at you. I was simply looking for somewhere to spin a web. I'm sorry I frightened you."

"That's all right," said Teddy Robinson.

"I believe I do make funny faces when I'm thinking," said the spider. "I often seem to frighten people without meaning to. Have you heard about Miss Muffet? Well, I gave her such a fright that they've been making a song about it ever since; but it was quite by mistake, you know."

Teddy Robinson began to feel rather sorry for the spider who was always frightening people without meaning to, so he said, "Well, *I'm* not frightened of you. I'm pleased to see you."

"Have you come to live here?" asked the spider.

"Oh, I hope not," said Teddy Robinson. "I mean I'm really only here by mistake. Deborah's sure to come and find me in the morning. She wouldn't have forgotten me tonight if she hadn't been given a Beautiful Present."

"What was it?" asked the spider.

"Bubbles," said Teddy Robinson. "They were very

pretty, but they kept bursting."

"And did you have a Beautiful Present too?"

"No," said Teddy Robinson sadly.

"What a shame," said the spider. "You know, I could make you a Beautiful Present myself. It wouldn't last very long, but it would last longer than a bubble."

"Could you really?" said Teddy Robinson.

"Yes," said the spider. "I could spin a web for you. I make rather beautiful webs, and they look lovely with the light shining on them."

"Oh, thank you," said Teddy Robinson. "I should like that. Will I be able to take it away with me?"

"Yes," said the spider. "But I must be careful not to join it to the wall or it will break when you move."

"And don't join it to the bicycle basket either, will you?" said Teddy Robinson. "I don't usually live in that."

"I see," said the spider. "Well, I will start at your ear, and go down here, and along here, and I'll catch the thread to your foot if you're sure that doesn't tickle you?"

"Yes, that will be very nice," said Teddy Robinson. "Shall I sing to you while you work?"

"Oh, do," said the spider. "I love music while I work."

So Teddy Robinson began singing:

"Spin, little spider, spin,
in and out and in."

And as he sang he heard a gentle whirring noise quite close to his ear, and knew that the spider had started spinning the web that was to be his Beautiful Present.

Soon the gentle noise of the spider spinning made Teddy Robinson so drowsy that he forgot to sing any more, and a little while afterwards he fell fast asleep.

It was morning when he woke up again. Someone was just opening the tool-shed door, and as the sunshine came streaming in Teddy Robinson could see the silver thread of the spider's web reaching right down to his toes. He kept very still so as not to break it.

Daddy had come to fetch his bicycle. As soon as he saw Teddy Robinson he called Deborah. She *was* surprised to see him.

"I thought we'd left you at Granny's!" she said. "Oh, you poor boy!"

"Yes, but look what he's got!" said Daddy.

"Oh, how lovely!" said Deborah, and she called

—reaching right down to his toes

Mummy to come and see. And Mummy and Daddy and Deborah all crowded round the bicycle to look at Teddy Robinson and admire his beautiful web.

"A spider must have made it in the night," said Daddy.

"Look how it sparkles in the sun!" said Mummy.

"And Teddy Robinson has got a Beautiful Present all of his own!" said Deborah.

Then Teddy Robinson was lifted very carefully out of the bicycle basket, and Deborah carried him into the house, holding him in front of her with both hands, so as not to break a single thread of the web.

"What happened to *your* Beautiful Present?" asked Teddy Robinson.

"It's finished. I threw away the tin," said Deborah.

"And where are all the bubbles?"

"Gone," said Deborah. "They all burst. Your web won't last for ever either. Nothing does."

"Except me," said Teddy Robinson. "It's a good thing *I* don't burst, isn't it?"

And that is the end of the story about
Teddy Robinson and the Beautiful Present.

– 12 –

Teddy Robinson Tries to Keep Up

One day Teddy Robinson was sitting in Deborah's window, looking across the road, when he suddenly saw something very odd. In the window of the house opposite he saw himself looking out.

"Fancy that," said Teddy Robinson, "I never knew I was reflected in that window." And he sat up a little straighter and began to admire himself quietly.

"My fur looks better than I thought," he said to himself. "The part that's been kissed away all round my nose hardly shows from here. And my trousers aren't too shabby at all. I'm really quite a handsome bear from a distance." And he was pleased to think the people over the road had such a fine view of him.

But a little later, when he looked across again, he had another surprise. He could see quite clearly in the reflection of the window opposite that he had a hat on. A large, round, red beret with a bobble on top.

"That's funny," he said to himself. "I don't remember Deborah putting my hat on. Anyway my hat doesn't look like that. Can she have bought me a new one, and put it on my head when I wasn't looking?" Just then Deborah came running in.

"Hallo," said Teddy Robinson. "Why have I got this hat on?"

"What hat?" said Deborah, surprised.

"Haven't I got a hat on?" said Teddy Robinson. "A large, round, red beret with a bobble on top?"

"No, of course you haven't," said Deborah, and she came over and looked at him closely.

"Look over there, then," said Teddy Robinson.

"Isn't that me?" And haven't I got a hat on?"

Deborah looked. "Oh, that's funny!" she said. "They've got a teddy bear just like you! He's even got the same sort of trousers. I wonder why they put him up in the window."

"Was it to show off that hat?" said Teddy Robinson.

"Yes, perhaps it was," said Deborah. "That big girl, Pauline Jones, lives there. The one who goes to school and wears a uniform. That's her hat."

"It's a very nice hat," said Teddy Robinson.

— a large, round, red beret with a bobble on top.

"Yes," said Deborah, "but I wish the girl was nice too. She's not a bit friendly. Once when I took you out in the dolls' pram she stared hard, but she never even smiled at us. When *I* go to a big school with a uniform I shan't be like that. I'll say hallo to everybody, no matter how young they are."

Teddy Robinson stared across at the other bear.

"I'd better have my hat on," he said.

"Yes, they may as well see you've got one too," said Deborah, and she fetched his knitted bonnet.

"Where are my other hats?" said Teddy Robinson.

"You haven't any, you know that," said Deborah. "But this is lovely, it's a real baby's bonnet."

"Yes, I was afraid it was," said Teddy Robinson. "Can't you lend me one of yours?"

So Deborah fetched one of her own hats. It had poppies and corn round it, and ribbon streamers.

"That's much better!" said Teddy Robinson. "Now, haven't I got a paper sunshade as well?"

"Oh, yes!" said Deborah. "What fun!"

And a few minutes later Teddy Robinson was sitting proudly in the window, with Deborah's best hat on and his paper sunshade over his head.

—sitting proudly in the window

Deborah was just having tea when she heard Teddy Robinson shouting, "Can I have something to eat? That bear over the road has got an orange!"

She ran in with her slice of bread and butter. It had a big bite taken out of it. She propped it up on Teddy Robinson's paw against the window, then went back to finish her tea. But a moment later Teddy Robinson called out again.

"Hey! That Jones bear has got a bun now!"

Deborah ran in again, this time with a slice of cake in her hand. She propped it up on his other paw.

"Now are you happy?" she said.

"Oh, yes, thank you," said Teddy Robinson.

But when Deborah came back again after tea, Teddy Robinson was looking gloomy.

"*Now* what's the matter?" she said.

"I don't like tea with nothing to drink," said Teddy Robinson.

Deborah looked across at the other window and saw that the Jones bear now had a bottle of milk in front of him, with a straw sticking out of it.

"Oh dear," she said, "poor Teddy Robinson! I'd better get the dolls' tea set out."

And soon Teddy Robinson was sitting with his tea nicely laid out in front of him on a tray.

"This *is* fun!" said Deborah. "I do wonder who is

doing it. Surely it can't be that girl, Pauline, who never even says hallo?"

Teddy Robinson didn't know who it was either. He tried to keep watch to see if he could see anyone moving about, but somehow he always just missed it.

Next time he looked he saw that the milk bottle had gone, and the bear was now reading a book.

"Bring me a book, Deborah!" he shouted. "A big book. The biggest you can find!"

Deborah came running in with the telephone book and propped it up in front of him on the toy blackboard. It was very dull, with nothing but long lists of names in it, but luckily Teddy Robinson couldn't read, so he didn't know how bored he was. And it was fun trying to keep up with the other bear.

"He doesn't even know I can't read," he said, and chuckled to himself.

But by bedtime he was getting quite stiff.

"Thank goodness I can get down now," he said. Then he looked across at the other house. A big dolls' cot had just been put on the window sill!

"Oh, my goodness!" he said, "whatever next?" Then he shouted loudly, "A bed! Bring me a bed!"

Deborah came running. "What is it now?"

"I must have a bed!" said Teddy Robinson. "A

bed all to myself. At once!"

"That's not a very nice way to ask," said Deborah.

"Please, dear Deborah, may I have a bed all of my own?" said Teddy Robinson. "I can't possibly let that Jones bear know I haven't got one."

Deborah rummmaged in the toy-cupboard and pulled out an old dolls' bed. "It's too small," she said.

"And the bottom's fallen out," said Teddy Robinson.

"But it's all we've got," said Deborah.

"Then it'll have to do," said Teddy Robinson. "Put my nightie on quickly and squeeze me in."

So Deborah did. Then she covered him with a doll's blanket, put the telephone book underneath, to stop him falling through, and put him up on the sill.

"Are you comfy?" she said.

"No, thank you," said Teddy Robinson. "But at least I'm glad I've got a proper nightie, and don't have to go to bed in my trousers."

"I wonder if they can see it," said Deborah.

"Shall we hang my trousers up?" said Teddy Robinson. "Then they'll know I haven't got them on."

So Deborah found a dress hanger, and hung Teddy Robinson's trousers up in the window for everyone to see. And Teddy Robinson lay underneath and thought

*—and thought how funny they looked
without him inside them—*

how funny they looked without him inside them.

Then Deborah kissed him and got into her own bed. Usually Teddy Robinson slept there too. Sometimes he pushed his way down in the night until he was right at the bottom of the bed and as warm as toast. But tonight he was very cold. The blanket was far too small, and he couldn't move an inch.

He had a dreadful night.

When at last Deborah came for him in the morning, he was too stiff and sleepy to sit up straight.

But Deborah was very bright. She said, "Oh, do look! The Jones bear is having breakfast now!"

Sure enough, there he sat in the window with a big packet of cornflakes in front of him.

"I'd better have eggs and bacon then, hadn't I?" said Teddy Robinson, waking up.

"No," said Deborah, "let's pretend you had breakfast in bed. Then while I'm having mine, you can be thinking of something to do afterwards."

But when she came back after breakfast Teddy Robinson was sitting all humped up, and she could tell by the look of his back that he was feeling sad.

"Haven't you thought of anything?" she said.

"No," said Teddy Robinson, "and I'm not going to. I'm tired of trying to keep up with the Joneses. They go too quickly for me. Look over there now."

Deborah looked across and saw that the Jones bear was now wearing a shiny blue party dress with big puffed sleeves, and a blue satin ribbon, tied in a bow between the ears.

"Oh dear," she said, "we haven't anything as grand as that. Shall I put on your best purple dress?"

"No," said Teddy Robinson sadly. "Did you see what he's got beside him?"

Deborah looked again. "Oh! A dear little dolls' sewing machine! *Aren't* they lucky?"

"Turn me round," said Teddy Robinson. "I shan't look any more. I think he's showing off. I don't like bears who put on airs." And he began singing, with his back to the window.

> *"Teddy bears*
> *who put on airs*
> *are not the the bears for me.*
> *Bears are best*
> *not over-dressed —*
> *in pants, perhaps,*
> *or just a vest,*
> *but* not *the clothes you wear for best —*
> *they're better fat and free.*
>
> *A friendly, free-and-easy bear,*
> *a cosy, jolly, teasy bear*
> *is always welcome*
> *everywhere.*
> *Fair and furry,*
> *fat and free,*
> *that's the kind of bear to be.*
> *Like me."*

After that he stuck his tummy out again and began to feel better.

"Lift me down," he said to Deborah. "If that Jones bear only wants to see what things I've got, then he doesn't need to see *me* at all. We can leave all my things in the window for him to look at, and then go off on our own to a desert island and be very happy with nothing at all. Why didn't I think of it before?"

So quickly they arranged all his things in the window. They hung up his nightie, his best purple dress and his trousers on three little dress hangers. They hung his paper sunshade and his knitted bonnet from the window latch. Then they took a sheet of cardboard and Deborah wrote on it in big black letters,

GONE AWAY FROM IT ALL

and they propped it up in front of the window on the toy blackboard. Then they went away.

Hours later Teddy Robinson was lying on his back in the middle of a small round flower-bed in the garden. He had no clothes on at all, and a gentle breeze ruffled the fur on his tummy. He sighed happily, staring up at the lupins as they waved gently over his head, and sang to himself softly,

> *"Lucky bear,*
> *lucky bear,*
> *all alone*
> *and free as air.*
> *No more things*
> *to bother me,*
> *lucky me,*
> *lucky me.*
> *Free-and-easy,*
> *fat and free,*
> *what a lucky bear I be . . ."*

"All the same," he said to himself, "I wish I had somebody else to be all alone and lucky with. That Jones bear would have done, if only he hadn't been so proud, showing off with all his things."

Just then he heard Mummy calling to Deborah.

"Listen," she said, "I've just met Mrs Jones who lives opposite, and what do you think she said? She

174

asked me why Teddy Robinson had gone away! I told her he hadn't, and she said, 'Well, that's funny, my Pauline said he had, and she's so sad about it.'"

"But why is she sad?" said Deborah.

"Mrs Jones says Pauline is very shy and finds it hard to make friends," said Mummy. "She's often seen you two together and wanted to talk to you, but she was too shy. Then when her birthday came she asked for a teddy bear like yours. Mrs Jones thought she was too old for it now she goes to a big school. But Pauline wanted it so much that she bought her one. And she says she has been so happy playing with you and Teddy Robinson, and she'd hoped you were going to be friends. Isn't it funny?"

Then Deborah told Mummy all about it. And a little later she went over to Pauline's house.

Teddy Robinson said, "Fancy that!" to himself three times over, and fell asleep in the sunshine.

When he woke up again, Deborah and Pauline were peering down at him through the lupins.

"There he is," said Deborah. "Don't tell, but this is his desert island. Let's put Teddy Jones down with him, then they can get to know each other."

So Teddy Jones had his party dress taken off and was put down beside Teddy Robinson. Then Pauline and Deborah ran off to play.

The two teddy bears lay on their backs and looked at each other sideways.

"Nice to lie down, isn't it?" said Teddy Robinson.

"*Very* nice," said Teddy Jones, with a cosy grunt.

"I must say I got a bit stiff sitting up in that window," said Teddy Robinson.

"So did I," said Teddy Jones. "This is a nice little place you've got here."

"Yes, it's my desert island," said Teddy Robinson. "Have you got one?"

"Oh, don't start all that again!" said Teddy Jones. "I'm worn out trying to keep up with you!"

"What!" said Teddy Robinson. "You can't be as worn out as I am. That's why I'm lying here. I nearly broke my back in that awful little bed."

"You may as well know I wasn't as comfortable as I looked," said Teddy Jones. "That cot was too small. I had a shocking night."

"*Did* you?" said Teddy Robinson. "Oh, I *am* glad! But I bet mine was worse; my bed had no bottom to it."

"Now I'll tell *you* something," said Teddy Jones. "That hat wasn't mine. I borrowed it."

"Mine wasn't mine either," said Teddy Robinson. "I only borrowed it to keep up with you."

"But why?" said Teddy Jones. "Fancy a proud sort

of chap like you trying to keep up with me!"

"*I'm* not a proud sort of chap," said Teddy Robinson. "I thought you were. I'm only me."

"And I'm only me," said Teddy Jones.

"Well now, isn't that nice?" said Teddy Robinson. "If you're only you and I'm only me, we don't have to bother any more."

"And we might even come to tea with each other instead?" said Teddy Jones.

...we don't have to bother any more."

"Yes, of course!" said Teddy Robinson. "What a silly old sausage of a bear I am! I've been so busy trying to show off to you with all the things I haven't got, that I quite forgot to make friends with you. You come to tea with me today, and I'll come to tea with you tomorrow."

So they did.

*And that is the end of the story about how
Teddy Robinson tried to keep up with the Joneses.*

– 13 –

Teddy Robinson
and the Band

One day Teddy Robinson and Deborah and Mummy all went off to spend the afternoon in the park.

When they got there Mummy found a comfortable seat to sit on and settled down to knit. Deborah and Teddy Robinson sat down on the other end of the seat and looked around to see what they could see.

Not far away some children were skipping on the grass. After she had watched them for a little while Deborah said, "I think I'd like to go and skip with those children, Teddy Robinson. You wouldn't mind staying here with Mummy, would you?

And Teddy Robinson said, "No, I don't mind. I don't care about skipping myself, but you go. I'll watch you."

So Deborah ran off to join the other children on the grass, and Teddy Robinson and Mummy stayed sitting on the seat in the sunshine.

Soon a lady came along, holding a very little boy by the hand. As soon as she saw Mummy the lady said, "Oh, how nice to meet you here!" And she sat down beside her and started talking, because she was a friend of hers.

The very little boy, whose name was James, stared hard and said nothing.

"Look, James, this is Teddy Robinson," said Mummy. "Perhaps you would like to sit up beside him and talk to him."

So James climbed up on the seat, and he and Teddy Robinson sat side by side and looked at each other, but neither of them said a word. They were both rather shy.

Mummy and the lady talked and talked and were very jolly together, but James and Teddy Robinson sat and did nothing and were rather dull together.

After a while James grew tired of sitting still, so he climbed down off the seat, and when nobody was looking he lifted Teddy Robinson down too, and toddled away with him.

"I hope you aren't going to lose us," said Teddy Robinson. But James said nothing at all.

They hadn't gone far before they came to some trees, and on the other side of the trees they saw a

—rather dull together—

bandstand with rows of chairs all round it. It was like a little round summerhouse, with open sides and a roof on top.

James and Teddy Robinson went over to look at it, and, as there was nobody there, they were able to go right up the steps and look inside. After that they ran in and out along the rows of empty chairs, until they came to the back row, just under the trees. Then James sat Teddy Robinson down on one of the

—just sitting there thinking

chairs, and sat himself down on the one next to him.

"I'm glad I've got a chair to myself," said Teddy Robinson. "It would be a pity to share one when there are so many."

But James didn't like sitting still for long. A moment later he got up again, and, forgetting all about Teddy Robinson, he ran back to the seat where Mummy and the lady were still talking. He was only a very little boy.

Teddy Robinson didn't mind at all. He felt rather grand sitting there all by himself on a chair of his own, with rows and rows of empty chairs standing all round him, and he began to think how nice it would be if someone should happen to pass by and notice him.

He looked up into the leafy branches over his head, so that people would think he was just sitting there thinking, and wouldn't guess that he had really been left there by mistake. And then he began thinking of all the things that people might say to each other when they saw him.

> *"Look over there!*
> *Look where?*
> *Why, there.*
> *Take care, don't stare,*
> *but alone on that chair*
> *there's a teddy bear!*
> *I do declare!*
> *A bear on a chair*
> *with his head in the air!*
> *How* *did* *he get there?"*

He said this to himself several times over, and then he went on:

"You can see that he's thinking
(not preening or prinking,
or winking or blinking,
or prowling or slinking,
or eating or drinking),
but just sitting thinking . . ."

But he didn't think this was very good, and any-way he was getting into rather a muddle with so much thinking about thinking. So he was quite pleased when suddenly there was a rustling in the leaves over his head, and a sparrow hopped along the branch nearest to him and stared down at him with bright, beady eyes.

"Good afternoon," chirped the sparrow. "Are you waiting for the music?"

"Good afternoon," said Teddy Robinson. "What music?"

"The band," said the sparrow. "I thought perhaps you had come to sing with the band. It always plays here in the afternoons."

"Oh," said Teddy Robinson, "how very nice that will be! I love singing."

"So do I," chirped the sparrow. "We all do. There are quite a lot of us up in this tree, and we sing with the band every afternoon. I really don't know how

"Are you waiting for the music?"

they would manage without us. I'm sure people would miss us if we didn't join in."

"How very jolly!" said Teddy Robinson. "When will the music begin?"

"Oh, very soon now," said the sparrow. "You'll see the chairs will soon begin to fill up, and then the band will arrive. Have you paid for your chair?"

"Oh, no," said Teddy Robinson. "Do I have to pay? I don't want to buy it, only to sit in it for a little while."

"Yes, but you have to pay just to sit in it," said the sparrow. "The ticket-man will be along in a minute. You'd better pretend to be asleep."

But Teddy Robinson was far too excited to pretend to be asleep. He was longing for the band to come and for the music to begin.

Before long one or two people came along and sat down in chairs near by; then two or three more people came, and after that more and more, until nearly all the rows of chairs were full. Several people looked as if they were just going to sit down in Teddy Robinson's chair, but they saw him just in time and moved on.

Then along came the ticket-man. Teddy Robinson began to feel rather worried when he saw all the people giving him money for their seats. But it was quite all right; the man came up to where he was sitting and stopped for a moment, then he smiled at Teddy Robinson and said, "I suppose it's no use asking *you* to buy a ticket," and went away.

Teddy Robinson was very glad.

"Was it all right?" asked the sparrow, peeping through the leaves.

"Yes," said Teddy Robinson. "I don't know how he knew I hadn't any money, but it's very nice for me, because now everyone will think I paid for my chair."

He sat up straighter than ever, and started to have a little think about how nice it was, to be sitting in a chair and looking as though you'd paid for it:

"Look at that bear!
He's paid for a chair;
no wonder he looks so grand;
with his paws in his lap,
what a sensible chap!
He's waiting to hear the band."

And then the band arrived. The men wore red and gold uniforms, and they climbed up the steps to the bandstand, carrying their trumpets and flutes and a great big drum.

"Here they come!" chirped the sparrow from the tree. "I must go and make sure the birds are all ready to start singing. Don't forget to join in yourself if you feel like it. Do you sing bass?"

"I don't know what that means," said Teddy Robinson.

"Rather deep and growly," said the sparrow.

"Oh, yes, I think perhaps I do," said Teddy Robinson.

"Good," said the sparrow. "We birds all sing soprano (that means rather high and twittery). We could do with a good bass voice." And he flew back into the tree again.

Then the band began to play.

The music went so fast that at first Teddy Robinson hadn't time to think of any words for it, so he just hummed happily to himself, and felt as if both he and the chair were jigging up and down in time to the music. Even the flies and bees began buzzing, and the birds were chirping so merrily, and the band was playing so loudly, that soon Teddy Robinson found some words to sing after all. They went like this:

> *"Trill-trill-trill*
>   *goes the man with the flute,*
>   *and the man with the trumpet*
>   *goes toot-toot-toot.*
> *Cheep-cheep-cheep*
>   *go the birds in the trees,*
>   *and buzz-buzz-buzz*
>   *go the flies and the bees.*
> *Mmmm-mmmm-mmmm*
>   *goes the teddy bear's hum,*
>   *and boom-boom-boom*
>   *goes the big bass drum."*

When the music stopped everyone clapped hard;

Then the band began to play.

but Teddy Robinson didn't clap, because, as he had been singing with the band, he was afraid it might look as if he were clapping himself.

He was just wondering whether he ought to get up and bow, as the leader of the band was doing, when he suddenly saw Deborah walking along between the rows of chairs.

She *was* surprised when she saw Teddy Robinson sitting among all the grown-up people.

"*However* did you get here?" she said. "And why didn't I know? And fancy you having a chair all to yourself!"

"What a pity you didn't come before!" said Teddy Robinson. "I've just been singing with the band. Did you hear everyone clapping?"

"Yes," said Deborah, "but I'd no idea they were clapping for you. I thought it was for the band."

"Me *and* the band," said Teddy Robinson, "and the sparrows as well. They've been singing quite beautifully."

"I *am* sorry I missed it," said Deborah. "I was skipping with the other children when somebody said the band had come, and I came over to see. I thought you were still sitting on the seat with Mummy."

"James and I got tired of it," said Teddy Robinson,

"so we came over here, and then James went back, so I stayed by myself. But you haven't missed all of it. Let's stay together and hear some more."

Then Teddy Robinson moved up so that Deborah could share his chair.

"I do think you're a clever bear," she said. "I always knew you could sing nicely, but I never thought I should find you singing with a proper band and with everyone clapping you!"

And that is the end of the story about
Teddy Robinson and the band.

14

Teddy Robinson
and Toby

O ne day Teddy Robinson and Deborah were just coming home from the shops when a lady called Mrs Peters came out of her house and gave Deborah a parcel.

"This is a present for your favourite doll," she said. "Open it when you get home."

"Oh, thank you," said Deborah. "What is it?"

"It's a surprise," said Mrs Peters. "I made it myself."

Deborah and Teddy Robinson ran home with the parcel.

"It's for you, Teddy Robinson," said Deborah. "I know you're not a doll, but you are my favourite, so it must be for you."

"I wonder what it is," said Teddy Robinson.

As soon as they got home Deborah undid the parcel. Inside the brown paper there was some white tissue paper, and inside the tissue paper lay a beautiful little ballet frock. It was white, with lots and lots of frills, and instead of sleeves it had shoulder straps with tiny pink roses sewn on them.

"Oh!" said Deborah. "It's just what I've always wanted – a dress with a skirt that really goes out. Oh, you *are* lucky!"

"But I'm not at all surc it's what *I've* always wanted," said Teddy Robinson. "I was rather hoping it would be a pair of Wellington boots."

"But you can't go to a party in Wellington boots," said Deborah.

"But I aren't going to a party," said Teddy Robinson.

"Yes, you are," said Deborah. At least, I am. I'm going to Caroline's party this afternoon, and now

"I'm not at all sure it's what I've always wanted"

193

you've got such a lovely dress you must come too."

"Was I invited?" said Teddy Robinson.

"Not really," said Deborah, "but that's the best of being a teddy bear – you can go to parties without being asked."

They tried on the dress, and it fitted Teddy Robinson perfectly. As soon as he saw the frilly skirt standing out all round him he felt so dainty and fairy-like that he forgot to be sorry any more that his surprise hadn't been a pair of Wellington boots.

"I see what you mean about a skirt that goes out all round," he said. "It does make you feel like dancing. Do you think if I practised I could learn to stand on one leg like a real ballet dancer?"

"I think you might," said Deborah. "Lean up against the window and see."

So Teddy Robinson stood on one leg, propped up against the window, and spent the rest of the morning thinking about how nice it was to be a ballet-dancing bear with roses on his braces. He rather hoped that people going by in the road outside might look up and see him.

"Perhaps they will think I am a famous dancing bear already," he said to himself, and he began making up a little song about it.

a ballet-dancing bear with roses on his braces

"Look at that bear
in the window up there
with the roses all over his braces!

You can see at a glance
how well he can dance,
and how charmingly pretty his face is!

What a beautiful dress!
I should say, at a guess,
he has danced in a number of places."

195

"But they're not braces," said Deborah. "They're shoulder straps, and anyway you can't dance as well as all that, even if you are standing on one leg."

When it was time to get ready for Caroline's party Teddy Robinson suddenly felt shy.

"Perhaps I won't go after all," he said.

"Why ever not?" said Deborah.

"Well, I do feel a bit soppy," said Teddy Robinson. "And I'm so afraid someone may ask me to dance. I haven't really practised enough yet. I wouldn't mind if I had some Wellington boots to wear as well. Nobody would expect me to dance then."

"But even if you had," said Deborah, "you'd have to leave them in the bedroom with the hats and coats. Nobody ever wears Wellington boots with a ballet frock."

"Couldn't I stay in the bedroom with the hats and coats?" said Teddy Robinson.

"All right," said Deborah, "you can if you want to."

So when they got to Caroline's house they went upstairs to take off their things, then Deborah went downstairs to the party, and Teddy Robinson stayed sitting on the bed among all the hats and overcoats and mufflers. He recognized some of them and began to feel rather sorry to be missing the party.

"That's Mary-Anne's blue coat with the velvet on the collar," he said to himself. "I wonder if she's brought Jacqueline with her." (Jacqueline was Mary-Anne's beautiful doll.) "And that's Philip's duffel coat. I shall be sorry not to see him. And that's Andrew's overcoat and yellow muffler. Oh, dear, I wish I'd come in my trousers and braces, or my purple dress."

Just then there was a scuffling noise outside the door, and Caroline's little dog, whose name was Toby, came rushing into the room and scrambled under the bed.

Teddy Robinson was very surprised. He didn't like Toby much because he was rough and noisy and thought he was a lot cleverer than anyone else. Teddy Robinson wondered whether someone was chasing Toby and waited to see what would happen. But nothing happened. Nobody else came into the room, and Toby stayed under the bed without making a sound, so after a while Teddy Robinson forgot about him and began singing to himself quietly:

"Parties are jolly and noisy
for children and musical chairs,
but bedrooms are quiet and cosy
for overcoats, mufflers, and bears."

"Who's that singing?" barked Toby, coming out from under the bed. "Oh, it's you," he said when he saw Teddy Robinson looking down at him. "Are you allowed up there?"

"Yes, I think so," said Teddy Robinson.

"I suppose it's because you're a visitor," said Toby. "I'm never allowed on the beds. But, then, you're only a teddy bear. I'm glad I'm not a teddy bear. I don't think much of them myself. Caroline has one, but she likes me much better."

"Yes, but hers is only knitted," said Teddy Robinson. "I'm a real teddy bear."

"Are you?" said Toby. "I can't see much difference.

"Are you allowed up there?"

Why are you wearing that peculiar dress?"

Teddy Robinson didn't know what 'peculiar' meant, but he guessed it was something rude, so he said, "It's not. It's a ballet-dancer's dress, and it's very pretty."

"It's pretty peculiar, you mean," said Toby. "And why are you wearing a ballet-dancer's dress if you're not dancing?"

"I'm resting just now," said Teddy Robinson.

"Yes, I see you are," said Toby. "But why aren't you going to the party?"

Teddy Robinson didn't like to say "Mind your own business" in somebody else's house, so he didn't say anything. He thought Toby was very rude and wished he would go away. But Toby went on talking.

"I think it's silly," he said, "to come to a party all dressed up, and then to stay upstairs on the bed."

"And I think it's silly to leave a party and come upstairs to go *under* the bed," said Teddy Robinson. "Why are you hiding?"

"I shan't tell you, unless you'll tell me," said Toby.

"All right," said Teddy Robinson. "You say first."

"They're going to have crackers," said Toby, "and I don't like the noise."

"Oh, I love things that go off with a bang!" said Teddy Robinson.

"Then why are *you* up here?" said Toby.

"I was afraid they might ask me to dance," said Teddy Robinson.

Just then Deborah came running in, all excited.

"Teddy Robinson, you must come down!" she said. "We're having tea, and we're going to have crackers, and I've told everybody about your ballet frock, and they all want to see it."

"All right," said Teddy Robinson, "but they won't ask me to dance, will they?"

"No," said Deborah. "You can just sit beside me and watch the fun."

So Teddy Robinson went down with Deborah, and everybody admired his ballet frock and made a fuss of him, and as nobody asked him to dance he sat beside Deborah at the table and felt very happy and pleased to be there after all.

When they pulled the crackers and they went *bang! bang! bang!* Teddy Robinson thought about Toby the dog hiding under Caroline's bed, and felt rather sorry for him.

But it serves him right, he thought. He was very rude to me, and, after all, I was a visitor, even if I wasn't invited.

One of Deborah's crackers had a tiny little silver shoe inside it. She hung it on a piece of ribbon and tied it round Teddy Robinson's neck. Then she gave him all the cracker papers and the little pictures off the outsides of the crackers, and Teddy Robinson sat on them to keep them safe. He had a lovely time.

After tea, when the children got down to play games, Teddy Robinson was put to sit on top of the piano so that he could watch all the fun.

They played Blind Man's Buff, and Squeak, Piggy, Squeak; and then Caroline's auntie sat down at the piano and said, "Now we'll have Musical Bumps, and there'll be a prize for the last person in."

This was very exciting. All the children shouted and laughed and jumped while Caroline's auntie played the piano very loudly. Then she stopped suddenly, and all the children had to sit down very quickly on the floor. Whoever was the last to sit down was out of the game.

The louder Caroline's auntie played the more the piano shook, until Teddy Robinson, sitting on top of it, felt he was simply trembling with excitement. The children went *jumpety-jump*, and Auntie went *thumpety-thump*, and Teddy Robinson went *bumpety-bump*, until at last only Philip and Caroline were left in the game. All the other children were sitting on the floor watching.

"This is the last go!" said Auntie, and she began

playing *Pop Goes the Weasel*. When she got to the "Pop!" she went *crash* on the piano with both hands and stopped playing. At the same minute Teddy Robinson bumped so high off the piano that he fell right in the middle of the carpet.

Philip was so surprised that he forgot to sit down at all. Everyone clapped their hands, and Auntie said, "Well done, Teddy Robinson! I really think you ought to have the prize. That was a wonderful jump, and you certainly sat down before Caroline did."

the wonderful jump

Caroline said, "Yes, Teddy Robinson ought to have the prize." And everyone else said, "Yes! Yes! Teddy Robinson is the winner!"

So Caroline's auntie gave him the prize, which was a giant pencil, almost as tall as himself. Teddy Robinson was very pleased.

After that the children all went off to a treasure hunt in the dining-room. Teddy Robinson sat in the big armchair and waited for them. He had a paper hat on his head, the silver-shoe necklace round his neck, his giant pencil on his lap, and the pile of cracker papers all round him. He was feeling very happy.

In a minute the door opened a little way and Toby's nose came round the corner, very close to the floor.

"Have they finished the crackers yet?" he asked.

"Yes," said Teddy Robinson. "You can come in now. They're having a treasure hunt in the dining-room."

"Oh, *are* they?" said Toby, and his nose disappeared again very quickly.

"Well, now," said Teddy Robinson, "I wonder why he rushed away like that. I told him it was quite safe to come in."

In less than two minutes Toby was back, but this

time he didn't just poke his nose round the door. He came trotting into the room, wagging his tail and holding a little flat parcel in his mouth.

"What have you got there?" said Teddy Robinson.

Toby dropped his parcel carefully on the floor.

"I won it in the treasure hunt," he said. "It's chocolate. I'm a jolly clever chap. Those silly children were all looking and looking, but I didn't even bother to look. I just walked in and sniffed my way up to it in a minute. Fancy not being able to smell a bar of chocolate! Don't you wish you were as clever as me?"

"I don't think you've noticed what I've got up here in the chair," said Teddy Robinson.

Toby stood on his hind legs and looked into the chair.

"My word!" he said. "Wherever did you get all those things?"

"From the party, before you came down," said Teddy Robinson. "These are from the crackers, and this is a little silver shoe, and this is the prize I won for Musical Bumps."

"Well, I never!" said Toby, looking at him with round eyes. "You seem to be a jolly clever chap too. I'm sorry I said what I did about teddy bears, and I'm sorry I was so rude about your dress."

"That's all right," said Teddy Robinson. "You

"Wherever did you get all those things?"

were wrong about teddy bears, but, you know, I rather agree with you about the dress. It is a bit soppy. I didn't want to hurt Deborah's feelings by not wearing it, but I'm glad I did now or I shouldn't have come to this lovely party. And now that I've won this very fine pencil I'm not going to bother to be a ballet dancer after all. I shall write a book instead."

And that is the end of the story about
Teddy Robinson and Toby.

15

Teddy Robinson is Put in a Book

One day Teddy Robinson sat in the bookshelf in Deborah's room. He had his thinking face on and his head on one side, because he was thinking very hard.

Deborah came running in to look for him.

"Where are you, Teddy Robinson?" she said, looking under the bed.

"I'm up here," he said. "You can't see me because I'm in the bookshelf, so I probably look like a book."

Deborah looked up and saw him. "You don't look like anything but my dear, fat, funny old bear," she said. "What are you doing up there?"

"Writing a book," said Teddy Robinson.

"I don't see you writing," said Deborah.

"No," said Teddy Robinson. "You know I can't write really. But I'm thinking, and it's the thinking that counts."

"And what are you thinking?"

"Well, I'm thinking that when I've finished thinking it would be nice if you would do the writing for me. You can use the giant pencil that I won at the party."

"Yes, I will," said Deborah. "That's a good idea. Tell me what the book is to be about."

"I don't know yet," said Teddy Robinson. "Come back later, when I've had time to think, and I'll tell you."

So Deborah went away, and Teddy Robinson started thinking again. But he just couldn't think *what* to put in his book. He thought of all the other people he had seen writing in books, and he began remembering the sort of things they mumbled to themselves while they were writing.

he just couldn't think what to put in his book

Mummy had a little book that she always wrote in before she went shopping, and her mumbling went something like this:

> *"A joint of bread,*
> *a loaf of lamb,*
> *a pound of eggs*
> *and some new-laid jam . . ."*

"Well, *that* doesn't make much sense," said Teddy Robinson to himself. Then he thought about the little book that Daddy sometimes wrote in when he came home at night. His mumbling went something like this:

> *"One-and-six,*
> *and two to pay,*
> *add them up*
> *and take them away . . ."*

"And that doesn't make sense either," said Teddy Robinson.

Then he remembered the little book that Auntie Sue used to write in when she was knitting. Her mumbling went like this:

"Two for purl
and two for plain,
turn them round
and start again.
Slip the stitch
and let it go,
drop the lot
and end the row . . ."

"That's no good either," thought Teddy Robinson. "It must be because they're grown-ups that they write such very dull books."

So then he thought about the books that Deborah liked to read to him. Their favourite was a book of nursery rhymes.

"All right," said Teddy Robinson to himself, "I'll write a book of nursery rhymes. Now, shall I start with

"Baa, baa, brown bear,
Have you any wool?

or

"Twinkle, twinkle, Teddy R.
How I wonder what you are?"

Just then Deborah came back and said, "Are you ready yet?"

"Listen," said Teddy Robinson. "How do you like this?

> "My *fur is brown, silly-silly.*
> Your *hair is green.*
> *When I am king, silly-silly,*
> *you shall be queen.*"

"Who are you calling silly?" said Deborah. "And my hair isn't green."

"What a pity," said Teddy Robinson, "because I could go on like that for ever."

"What do you really want to write about?" said Deborah. "What are you most interested in?"

"Me," said Teddy Robinson.

"Why, of course," said Deborah. "What a good idea! I know what we'll do. I'll put *you* in a book!"

"But would there be room for me between the pages? Shouldn't I get rather squashed?"

"No, I mean I'll make pictures and stories about you and put them in a book: then everyone will know about you and think how lucky I am to have such a beautiful bear."

"Oh, *yes*," said Teddy Robinson. "Will you have a

picture of me being a pirate?"

"Yes, and I'll tell about how you wanted to go to a party in a ballet frock and Wellington boots."

Deborah found the giant pencil in the toy-cupboard; then she went off to ask Mummy for enough paper to make a whole book. Mummy gave her a roll of drawer-paper.

While Deborah was away Teddy Robinson sat and thought about how jolly it was to be put in a book without having to bother to write it. He began to feel rather important and started talking loudly to the dolls inside the toy-cupboard.

"Wait till you see me in a book," he said. "Do you wish *you* were going in a book? *My* book is going to be the most beautiful and enormous book you ever saw. It will be made of red leather, with gold edges to the pages, and it will be as big as the garden gate."

"Don't be so silly," said Deborah, coming back with the paper. "It won't be anything of the sort, and you really mustn't talk like that or I shall wish I'd never thought of it. After all, lots of other bears have been in books before. What about Goldilocks? She had three of them."

"Yes," said Teddy Robinson, "but they were only pretend bears. It's different when you're a real bear. You can't help feeling proud."

Deborah began to unroll some of the paper and cut it up into pages for the book. But because the paper had been rolled up the pages were all curly and wouldn't lie flat. So Teddy Robinson sat on them to help flatten them out, and while he was waiting he sang a little song to himself, very quietly in case anyone should think he was showing off.

> *"There are books about horses,*
> *and books about dogs,*
> *and books about tadpoles,*
> *and books about frogs,*
> *and books about children;*
> *but wait till you see*
> *the wonderful, beautiful*
> *Book about Me."*

When the pages were flat enough Deborah folded them together like a real book. But some of them went crooked, so she had to cut the edges. Then the pages seemed too tall, so she cut the tops off them. Then they seemed too wide, so she cut the sides off them. But whichever way she cut them they kept on coming crooked, so in the end the book got smaller and smaller, and still it didn't look like a proper book at all.

"There's just one sheet left," said Teddy

... and still it didn't look like a proper book at all.

Robinson. "I'm sitting on it. Couldn't you put me in a newspaper instead?"

"No," said Deborah. "I want you in a book. I think we'd better go and ask Mummy about it."

But Mummy was busy hanging up curtains.

"I'm sorry I can't help you just now," she said, "but I don't think I should be much good at making a book anyway. Mr Vandyke Brown is the man you ought to ask. He's made lots and lots of books."

Teddy Robinson and Deborah both knew Mr Vandyke Brown because he lived in their road. He had white hair, and a very large black hat which he always took off whenever he met them out of doors. Teddy Robinson specially liked him because he always said, "And how are you, sir?" and shook his paw very politely after he'd finished saying "Good Morning" to Deborah.

"Let's go and see him now," whispered Teddy Robinson.

"Yes, I think we will," said Deborah.

So she brushed Teddy Robinson's fur, and off they went.

Mr Vandyke Brown opened the door himself when they rang the bell.

"Good morning," he said to Deborah. "What can I do for you? And how are you, sir?" he said to Teddy

Robinson, shaking him by the paw.

Deborah told him why they had come, and Mr Vandyke Brown looked hard at Teddy Robinson, with his head first on one side and then on the other. Then he said, "Yes, I see what you mean. He *would* look nice in a book. Come inside and let's talk about it."

So they all went indoors into Mr Vandyke Brown's sitting-room, which was very untidy and comfortable. Teddy Robinson sat on a little stool, Deborah sat in a large armchair, and Mr Vandyke Brown sat on a table and smiled at them both.

"Am I to do the pictures or the stories?" he asked.

"Well, it would be very nice if you'd do them both," said Deborah. "I could tell you the stories if you like."

"Yes," said Mr Vandyke Brown, thinking hard. "Now, what sort of pictures would you like?"

"What sort can we have?" asked Deborah.

"There are all sorts of different ways of making pictures," said Mr Vandyke Brown. "I wonder which would be best . . ."

"Ask him what sort of ways," whispered Teddy Robinson, leaning towards Deborah.

"Teddy Robinson wants to know what sort of ways," said Deborah.

—five little pictures of Teddy Robinson—

—one in wool, one in chalk,

"Well," said Mr Vandyke Brown, "drawing them, or painting them, or embroidering them with wool on cards, or chalking them on pavements, or sticking little coloured pieces of paper on to a bigger piece of paper—"

"I don't think chalking them on pavements would do," said Deborah, "because we'd never be able to lift them off. But I think any of the others might be nice."

"I'll tell you what," said Mr Vandyke Brown. "I'll do one of each kind; then you can choose which you like best."

So Mr Vandyke Brown made five little pictures of Teddy Robinson; one in wool, one in chalk, one with

one with pen and ink,
one with paint,
and one with bits of sticky paper

pen and ink, one with paint, and one with little bits
of sticky paper.

Teddy Robinson didn't like the sticky-paper one
or the wool one because it made him look rather
babyish, and Deborah didn't like the chalky one
because it made him look smudgy and unbrushed,
and neither of them liked the painted one because
the colours were so queer. But they both loved the
pen-and-ink one because it looked so like him.

"I'm glad you chose that one," said Mr Vandyke
Brown. "I hoped you wouldn't choose the painted
one, because those are the only colours left in my
paint box. All the others seem to have dried up. And
I hoped you wouldn't choose the chalky one, because

'Shall I look fierce?

Or shall I stand on my head?'

He kept wondering how he ought to look

I always get chalk all over my clothes. And I hoped you wouldn't choose the sticky-paper one, because when I sneeze all the little bits of paper get blown away. And I *am* glad you didn't choose the wool one, because I'm very bad at threading needles."

Teddy Robinson didn't understand a word of all this, but he knew it was his very own book that was being talked about, so he sat quite still and tried to look ordinary. Really he was feeling rather shy.

218

He kept wondering how he ought to look when Mr Vandyke Brown started drawing him.

"Shall I look fierce?" he said to himself. "Or shall I do something clever, like standing on my head? Or shall I just pretend I don't know he's drawing me?"

"I do want a picture of him with his party face on," said Deborah.

"Very well," said Mr Vandyke Brown. "And while I'm drawing him, suppose you do some drawing too."

So he gave Deborah a piece of paper and a pencil, and Deborah drew a picture of Mr Vandyke Brown

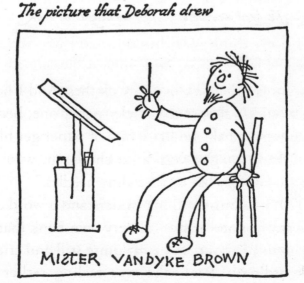

The picture that Deborah drew

MIƷTER VANDYKE BROWN

219

while Mr Vandyke Brown drew a picture of Teddy Robinson. And Teddy Robinson did nothing at all. He decided it would be better if he just went on looking ordinary.

For a whole week after that Teddy Robinson and Deborah went every day to Mr Vandyke Brown's house, and by the end of the week there were pictures of Teddy Robinson lying all over the room, and pages and pages of stories.

"I think we've got enough now to fill a book," said Mr Vandyke Brown, picking up the pages off the chairs and tables.

"But they're all on different-sized pieces of paper," said Deborah. "How shall we sew them together to make a book?"

"I don't think we'll bother," said Mr Vandyke Brown. "I hate sewing. And, anyway, I've got a better idea. Tomorrow I'll take them all to my friend, the Publisher. He is a very clever man who knows all about how to make proper books. If he likes these he will make them into a real book, so that anyone who wants it can buy it."

"Can we come too?" asked Deborah.

"I don't see why not," said Mr Vandyke Brown, "if Mummy says so. But you'll have to be very quiet and wait downstairs."

—pictures of Teddy Robinson lying all over the room.

So the very next day Teddy Robinson and Deborah went on a bus with Mr Vandyke Brown all the way to town to see the Publisher. At least Mr Vandyke Brown went to see the Publisher, and Teddy Robinson and Deborah sat downstairs in a large room where a lady was busy packing up big parcels of books.

They were so quiet that they never said a word to each other all the time they were waiting, and it seemed a very long time indeed. But at last Mr Vandyke Brown came leaping down the stairs, smiling all over his face, and hustled them out into the street.

"What happened?" asked Deborah as they hurried along.

"Let's go and eat some ices," said Mr Vandyke Brown, "and I'll tell you all about it."

So they went into a teashop and ate ices with chocolate sauce while Mr Vandyke Brown told them what had happened.

"The Publisher was very kind," he said. "He likes the book very much. He laughed in all the right places, and he hopes you didn't hurt yourself, Teddy Robinson, when you fell off the piano."

"But where is the book?" asked Deborah.

"Oh, it won't be ready for a long while yet," said

Mr Vandyke Brown. "I'm afraid we shall have to wait weeks and weeks before it is ready. It always takes a long time to make a real book. Is Teddy Robinson disappointed?"

"I think he is rather," said Deborah. "But never mind."

"Dear me," said Mr Vandyke Brown, "how silly of me not to have thought of it before! Did he think I should come down with the finished book in my hand?"

"He did really," said Deborah. "But never mind."

"Excuse me just a minute," said Mr Vandyke Brown, and he jumped up and ran to the door. Just outside, a lady was selling bunches of violets. Mr Vandyke Brown bought one and came hurrying back. Then he took off his large black hat, bowed low to Teddy Robinson, and gave him the bunch of violets.

"Please accept these with my most grateful thanks," he said.

Teddy Robinson didn't know what he was talking about, but he was very pleased indeed, because he had never been given a bunch of flowers all of his own, and nobody had ever bowed to him before in quite such an important way.

Weeks and weeks later, when they had nearly

forgotten all about it, a parcel came addressed to Master Teddy Robinson, and there inside was *his* book. It wasn't made of red leather, and it wasn't nearly as big as the garden gate, but Teddy Robinson thought it was the nicest book he had ever seen, because it had his very own name on the cover.

*And that is the end of the story about how
Teddy Robinson was put in a book.*